TAKE CARE OF MY GIRL

CAROL STANLEY

SCHOLASTIC BOOK SERVICES
New York Toronto London Auckland Sydney Tokyo

For my mother and father

Cover Photo by Owen Brown

ISBN: 0-590-32203-6

12 11 10 9 8 7 6 5 4 3 2 1   11   1 2 3 4 5 6/8

Printed in the U. S. A.   06

TAKE CARE OF MY GIRL

A Wildfire Book

WILDFIRE TITLES
FROM SCHOLASTIC

Love Comes to Anne by Lucille S. Warner
I'm Christy by Maud Johnson
That's My Girl by Jill Ross Klevin
Beautiful Girl by Elisabeth Ogilvie
Superflirt by Helen Cavanagh
A Funny Girl Like Me by Jan O'Donnell
Just Sixteen by Terry Morris
Suzy Who? by Winifred Madison
Dreams Can Come True
    by Jane Claypool Miner
I've Got a Crush on You by Carol Stanley
An April Love Story by Caroline B. Cooney
Dance with Me by Winifred Madison
One Day You'll Go by Sheila Schwartz
Yours Truly, Love, Janie by Ann Reit
The Summer of the Sky-Blue Bikini
    by Jill Ross Klevin
I Want to Be Me by Dorothy Bastien
The Best of Friends by Jill Ross Klevin
The Voices of Julie by Joan Oppenheimer
Second Best by Helen Cavanagh
A Kiss for Tomorrow by Maud Johnson
A Place for Me by Helen Cavanagh
Sixteen Can Be Sweet by Maud Johnson
Take Care of My Girl by Carol Stanley

Chapter 1

Kate sat in the last seat in the far row by the windows in Mr. Wagner's seventh period history class. Wagner was both near-sighted and forgetful, and so sitting in the back of his class meant you didn't get called on too often. Which was what Kate wanted — a little freedom to tune in when she wanted and when she didn't, to be able to write poems, or watch the snow fall out-side, or to just sit back and count the stains on Wagner's tie.

She was getting a little nervous lately, though. It had been an especially long time since Wagner had called on her, and she had the unlucky feeling her number was about to come up. And so today, she was making an effort to pay attention.

This was difficult even in the best of circumstances. Wagner was a nice enough guy and a pretty smart teacher. But if you listened to him for any length of time, you were sure to be either lulled into napland by his droning monotone, or driven crazy wondering how many sentences he could

1

start with his favorite verbal tic, "Henny-how."

Usually, Kate managed to keep her ears open enough to pick up her name and at least the last part of the question asked. (The system wasn't foolproof. A couple of weeks ago, she had figured out that he was looking for causes for a war. She popped up with "ice-free port," that being one of the causes for nearly every war they had studied in world history. Unfortunately, at that particular moment, Wagner was on the Boer War in South Africa, where ice was not a major concern.)

This afternoon, her plan to pay attention was complicated by the fact that she was already preoccupied with hating Stacy Adams — more specifically, with reworking the scene that had taken place that morning at their adjoining lockers.

Stacy didn't really have to do much to be hateable as far as Kate was concerned. Just existing was enough. All Kate had to do to set her top molars grinding against the bottom ones was think of one aspect or another of Stacy's golden-girl life. The clothes she wore months before all the other girls copied them. The way she could get out of practically any trouble just by flashing one of her 200-watt smiles. The way she turned up on the honor roll every semester, even though Kate knew for a fact

2

that she never brought a book home. The way she had Gary Conners walk her between every class and was dated up with him both nights of every weekend. (This last one was conjecture on Kate's part, but she figured it had to be true. It was impossible to imagine Stacy Adams sitting home on a Saturday night. Actually, it was impossible to imagine Stacy sitting home at all.)

On top of all this, Stacy, who managed to seem totally unaware of Kate most of the time, had fallen into a pattern of focusing in on her every morning at the lockers for just long enough to see if there was any possibility of sharpening her claws with a good dig. This morning she had gone too far.

Kate had decided to wear, for the first time, the ceramic dolphin pendant her parents had brought back for her from their trip to Mexico last month. Stacy must have zeroed in on it right away. Kate barely had her combination lock undone before she heard Stacy poking around in the depths of her locker, saying, "Something's certainly fishy around here. Must be a dead perch back here somewhere."

Kate hung up her coat, tossed her lunch on the shelf, pulled out her English book, slammed the door shut, and ducked into her homeroom. She didn't want to hang

3

around for what was sure to be another five minutes worth of Stacy's scintillating wit.

Now, though, she was running through all the possible snappy comebacks she could have made — those neat, double-edged ones that would have let her come off as cool and unflappable, while at the same time putting Stacy in her well-deserved place. It took her most of the seventh period, but she came up with three of them. All too late to do her any good, of course. It was the story of her life.

What was making her feel worse, though, was that during the first change of classes she had gone into the girls' john, taken off the pendant, and slipped it into her pocket. As much as she told herself that it was just to avoid taking any more flak for the rest of the day, she couldn't help feeling crummy. She couldn't avoid the fact that she was — in a small way — selling out her mother's taste to fit in with people like Stacy, who she didn't, or at least shouldn't, care about at all.

The problem was that, even if you knew you were right and they were wrong, people like Stacy were hard not to care about. Around school, they held court. What they said was listened to. What they did was imitated. If you didn't go along, if you didn't work very hard at being like them and liked *by* them, you didn't get talked

4

to in the halls, didn't get your lipstick borrowed, didn't get asked over to the McDonald's after school, or the basketball games on Friday night. And you got jokes made about your fish pendant.

Of course, if Stacy had worn the pendant, every girl in school would have had one within three weeks. It really was unfair.

Who cares? Kate thought, walking home from school. She wouldn't want to be in their dumb crowd if they begged her. Of course, she wouldn't have minded a crack at turning them down when they did come begging. Like when Stacy Adams would call to ask Kate to her pajama party and Kate would say she'd love to, but she already had a date that night with a college guy.

So far, real life hadn't come up with any juicy opportunities like that. Not that she was a friendless wonder like Barbara Ruckles, who snuck off at lunchtime to have a sandwich in the library stacks because, as she had told Kate, it disgusted her to go down to the cafeteria and eat at a table where five other people were chewing.

Kate was a little more social than that. At least she had a few friends. There were five of them in the group. If you could call it that. It wasn't as if they were a real tight clique or anything. Kate had the feeling that the rest of them, like her, all hung around with each other because it was better than being alone, and because it was something to do until something better came along.

Norma was the smartest, but she was sort of like a forty-five-year-old person inside a teenage body. Kate wished she could like Norma better, but it was hard getting close to someone who was always so serious and sensible, and whose main interest from one year to the next was winning the school science fair.

Bootsie was more fun, but so daffy and scatter-brained and always giggling even when nothing funny was going on. Anytime she was around Bootsie (who no one, not even the oldest teachers, ever bothered to call Beatrice) for more than an hour straight, Kate started feeling like someone had been thwanging away at her head with a small mallet.

If Bootsie didn't care about being called Bootsie, Andrea went to the opposite extreme of wincing whenever anyone dared to call her Andy. Andrea was like that about a lot of stuff. Her parents had money and a big house and a maid who filled Andrea's lunch bag with little, crustless sandwich triangles and apples already cut up into wedges. Andrea's house had a pool table and an electric corn popper, and Andrea's room had a real stereo with separate components. And so her house was the center for their getting together. Somehow Andrea had misconstrued this into the notion that everyone always came to her house because she was the leader of the pack. No one had the nerve to set her straight on this. Or maybe it was just that no one else cared enough about the pack to care who was the leader, and so they just let Andrea go along thinking she was. The problem was that all this assumed power also made her a little obnoxious. For instance, ever since last summer, when her parents had taken her on one, puny, three-week package tour of London, Paris, and Rome, she had felt compelled to lecture the rest of them on the wonders of belonging to the jet set and the cultural advantages of global travel.

"People who haven't been abroad," she would say to the rest of them, "simply can't have any true understanding of sophistication."

If Andrea were one tenth as cool as she thought she was, she would be really unbearable. As it was, being overweight and fairly homely and never having had a date and not being very well liked by most of the other kids all helped to keep her more or less in place.

Most of the time, Kate didn't pay much attention to her. Still, the next time Andrea told her she really ought to go to Continental Coiffures, that with a good haircut Kate would look so much less Midwestern, Kate was going to pop her one.

The best of the lot was Lucy, and even she left a lot to be desired. In the first place, it was hard to get very excited about a friendship based mainly on the fact that you had both lived on the same block for the past six years.

Lucy did have her good points. She was always more or less around, and willing to tag along for the things that were too boring or scary to do alone, like taking back library books, or going to the dentist. The other side of it was that Lucy was not exactly a thrill a minute to be with. She had the attention span of a fruit fly on anything but her two main preoccupations — the French horn, which she practiced two hours a day after school, and boys. This set up sort of a conversational roadblock between them because, if there was anything Kate knew less about than the French horn, it was the opposite sex.

On any other subjects, Lucy was maddeningly thick. When Kate had spilled the Stacy Adams story at lunch, Lucy listened to the whole thing (as intently as she could, given the fact that half of her attention during every lunch period was devoted to seeing if Ron Loedwick was looking at her), and then came up with: "Yeah, she thinks she's got it made. But she's the worst clarinet in the whole band."

Kate let it drop. It would have been cruel to point out that Stacy was probably taking band for an easy elective, and could probably care less if they yanked her clarinet away and gave her a kazoo.

That was just how it was with Lucy. You could count on her, but not really. Usually Kate didn't mind too much, but lately she wished she had someone around who was more real friend and less just filler. A lot of things were bumping around in her head. Not just why Stacy Adams got to her so badly, but other stuff. Like why Rick Padillo made her go so goofy and self-conscious just by brushing past her to get to his seat in Spanish. Rick Padillo, for heaven's sake. He wore the same crummy pair of tennis shoes every day and after three months, still said "Bwaynas *Die*-as."

Another thing was that she couldn't figure out why the school part of school was so easy for her and the non-school part so hard. She would have liked to have had someone to bounce these things off of, but nobody at Benton seemed a likely prospect.

About halfway home, her thoughts turned the corner along with her onto Morningside

Drive, where she lived. The worst part of the day was over and the best part was just three blocks away.

Her mother was supposed to get the material for Kate's new blazer today, and tonight they would cut the pattern. She knew her mom would be in the kitchen starting dinner, and so went around to the back door. She thought how it was one of the nice, small constants of life — that every day when she got home at 4:00, her mother would, for sure, be in the kitchen starting dinner. If one time she had even wandered off as far as the basement to put a load of clothes in the dryer or something, Kate would have been astounded.

It just wouldn't happen, though. Her mother was a very organized person. Mornings, she worked in the antique shop. On days when she did the laundry, she did it between noon and 2:00. Dusting and vacuuming got slipped in there somewhere, but always before 4:00 because at 4:00 her mother was always in the kitchen starting dinner.

Kate opened the back door.

"Hi, honey," her mother said.

"Hi. What are you fixing?"

"Just fried chicken. I'm not feeling very imaginative today. How'd it go at school?"

"Okay," Kate said, taking off her boots,

making sure to put them on the newspaper laid out next to the door.

"Just okay?"

"Fine. Really. We got our English papers back from Miss Dougherty."

"And you got an A."

"How'd you know?"

"Two ways. You always lead off with the best part. And you always get A's in English."

"Oh."

"But I still like to hear."

"What if I got a B once? Or a C? Would you be disappointed?"

"Of course. I'd know you hadn't been working hard enough."

"But I am."

"I know you are. Do you want some of that chocolate cake?"

"I'd better not. I'm putting on weight again. I don't want to have to get a size larger pattern for the blazer."

"Oh, honey."

"What?"

"I completely forgot."

"You didn't."

"It was a crazy, hectic day. I met Daddy for lunch, then I had to run out to the mall to pick up a few things."

"But the Fabric Mart's right on the way. I don't see how you could just forget."

"Kate. Stop it. I won't have you pouting. I was busy all day. It slipped my mind, and that's that. We'll just have to put it off a day or two. Are you sure you don't want a snack?"

"No thanks, I'll wait for dinner. I think I'll go up to my room. I've got a lot of homework."

Which was sort of a lie. Kate hardly ever had as much homework as she told her mother she did, and the couple of hours after dinner when her parents expected her to be at the kitchen table with her books open was usually more than enough time to get it done. But it was a good excuse to go up to her room after school. Mostly she spent the time napping — something her mother disapproved of as contributing to late bedtimes and bad sleeping habits — and reading novels, which her mother thought she did too much of instead of getting into group activities.

Kate's father didn't seem to care too much what she did with her spare time. She supposed if she ever got into something that involved breaking and entering, or the Hell's Angels, or taking his car out to the Demolition Derby, he might come down on her, but anything within her normal, boring range seemed to pass beneath his notice. Most of the problem was with her mother, who worried that Kate wasn't a normal teenager.

It was hard to get bothered too much by this, seeing as her mother's notion of a normal teenager was at least ten years out of date. Kate figured it was assembled from cartoons in her ladies' magazines and advice in the child psychology books she took out of the library from time to time.

For instance, from overhearing her mother in the living room with her friend Betty one day, Kate knew her mother worried that she didn't have the gang over until all hours to "spin platters," or hang on the phone forever, or belong to a fan club, or keep her room in a perpetual state of clutter.

"Not that I'd let her get away with much of that," she had told Betty, "but those kinds of problems would be easier to deal with. If she were running around all the time, I could just ground her. What do you do with a kid who's grounded herself?"

That last part had stopped Kate in her tracks. Not that she felt bad about never having done anything to get grounded. She didn't want to be bad. What made her feel crummy was realizing that if she ever did get grounded, it wouldn't make any significant difference in her social life.

Of course, one factor was that her

parents hadn't let her start dating yet. Well, that was sort of a lie. They had told her when she started high school that they didn't think she should date yet. Since then there hadn't really ever been an occasion to bring the subject up, so she didn't really know where they stood on the issue now. And there had already been two exceptions, if either of them counted as dates. The first was the big dance at the end of freshman year. Jimmy Murphy, who lived two doors down and whom she had known since they were both about four years old, told her his dad would give them both a lift over to the gym. When they got there, they had some punch and cookies and Jimmy asked her if she thought she had done all right on the history final, and she asked him if he still collected South American stamps. This about exhausted their conversational possibilities and so Jimmy wandered off and spent the rest of the dance talking to a bunch of guys against one wall. She hung around with her girlfriends against another wall, with three time outs for recombing her hair in the girls' john. At 11:00, Jimmy's father, who apparently was the only one who considered this a date, picked them up and took them out for a pizza.

The other time was when she went out

to dinner last year with her parents and some old friends of theirs from out of town. The friends had a son who was seventeen, and so he and Kate sort of got paired off for the night, with the four parents sniggering like crazy and thinking it was real cute. Her parents and the Robertsons went out for a drink after dinner and so the son, Rick, brought her home in his dad's car. He brought her up to the door and they fumbled around for a while and she finally decided to turn and go into the house just as he finally decided to kiss her good night, and so he wound up kissing the collar of her coat. It still embarrassed Kate whenever she thought about it.

Now, if anyone ever asked, she just said her parents hadn't let her start dating yet. It was less complicated than saying she had had one dumb date and one almost date and nothing since. And less embarrassing. This way it sounded like her parents were to blame, or at least that she wasn't pushing them because she was still waiting for the right moment or the right person.

This not having started dating yet, when most of the other kids had, was one of the ways Kate thought she wasn't a normal teenager, as opposed to the ways her mother thought she wasn't normal. Another was that she didn't have anything juicy enough going in her life to keep secrets from her parents. All her friends were always saying don't tell your parents anything, but she couldn't think of anything in her life that didn't seem safe enough to tell them. Except about her make-up.

Kate wasn't sure why she bought all the make-up she did. It sure ate a big hole in her allowance money and, since her mother thought she was too young for anything but light lipstick, she couldn't really wear it anywhere but around her room, carefully putting it on in front of the mirror after school, then taking it off with cold cream before she went down to dinner. From time to time, she would tell herself how dumb this was, resolve not to buy any more, then see in a magazine some new eyeshadow or lipstick that promised to be just the miracle needed to turn her from her drab self into a dead ringer for the model in the picture. And then she was hooked again.

She once thought of sending her picture off to a big eye make-up company. The one with the before and after models in its commercials. Every time she looked at herself in the mirror, she couldn't help but think she'd be perfect as the mousey girl in the ads who is Cinderella-ized into instant glamour through the wonders of modern cosmetics.

This afternoon, though, she didn't feel much like doing her face, even though she had just bought a new sable brown, fine-line eyeliner that looked especially promising. Nor did she really want to read or take a nap. What she most wanted to do, although she realized it wouldn't win her the Miss Congeniality title, was sulk.

It wasn't like her mother to forget something like the material. And not really her style to snap at Kate for being hurt that she had forgotten. Usually they got along real well and, as long as Kate was careful not to cross any of the lines her mother felt strongly about, were more like friends than like mother and daughter.

The other thing that bothered her was her mother mentioning having had lunch with Daddy. They had never had lunch together that Kate could remember. Maybe there was some trouble. Something they couldn't discuss around the house when she was there. Maybe something about her. But she couldn't think of anything. Maybe they were getting a divorce like Ellen Fisher's parents. But Kate didn't think so. Her parents never fought, and her dad always kissed her mother when he came in from work at night. Thy laughed at each other's jokes, and generally seemed to like each other just fine. Kate couldn't think of anything about them that resembled what people getting a divorce would act like.

Still, something did seem to be afoot. She lay down on her bed and stared at the ceiling a while trying to figure out what it might be, but fell asleep before she got very far.

At dinner, things seemed pretty normal. Her dad seemed a little abstracted — asking Kate to pass the butter when it was already in front of him — but that wasn't too unusual. He got like that whenever he was especially harried at work.

After dinner, Kate washed and dried the dishes, which was one of the regular chores she did in exchange for the allowance she wasted on make-up. It took her an especially long time because of the fried chicken, which left enough grease on the plates to make them tough to bring up to her mother's standards for what a clean plate should look like. When she was done, she brought her books down, and studied in the kitchen until nine, when she was allowed to watch TV for the two hours before her bedtime.

It was Thursday, when two of her favorite shows were on, and so she was particularly looking forward to settling down in front of the set with a glass of milk and the piece of chocolate cake she had decided to give in to.

By the time she got there, her parents were already watching the beginning of one of her shows, but when they saw her come in, they passed a look between themselves and her dad turned the set off. Since her dad never turned off the TV, falling asleep in front of it the nights her mother didn't get him to bed before he nodded off, Kate knew that she had been right this afternoon. Something definitely was up.

"Come in and sit down a minute. We have some exciting news for you," her mother said. "The company has decided to install computers in all of its branches, just like it did in Daddy's."

"That's the news?"

"Well, baby," her father said, "they need someone to oversee the whole thing. Since I'm the guy who started it, they figure they might as well let me follow through."

"He's being modest," her mother said. "It's a big step up. And there's going to be a much better job waiting when he's through with this troubleshooting. We've been waiting for a month to hear for sure about this."

"How many branches are there?"

"Seven."

"And you have to go to all of them? I mean, you couldn't do some of them by phone or something?"

"It's not that kind of deal, baby."

"You'll have to leave Mom and me alone here the whole time?"

"Not exactly."

"You mean we get to come along? Oh neat!"

"Hold on a second," her dad said. "Where would you go to school? Remember, I'm going to be making seven stops."

"I could just bring my books and study on my own."

"I don't think that would be good enough. We called Mr. Warlick this afternoon and he said they couldn't possibly let you out for such a long time and still give you credit. So I'm afraid this time it's going to have to be just your mother and me."

"You're going to leave me here alone? I don't think I can handle that. I'd have to buy all the groceries and I iron terribly. And I think I'd be scared at night."

"Now, baby, do you really think we'd just abandon you like that?"

"I guess not."

"Of course not. Your mother and I have it all figured out. We'll just get a big basket, wrap you in a blanket and stick you in it, then set you on the doorstep of the nearest convent."

"Your father's being funny. I called your Aunt Caroline tonight and it's all set. They'd love to have you. You can move there right after Christmas and finish up the school year there. Daddy should be finished sometime next summer. You can come home then and go back to Benton for your senior year."

"Well," said her father after about a three-minute silence, "aren't you going to say anything?"

"Could I go to the convent instead?"

Chapter 2

"**R**eally Kate," Lucy said, "I don't know what you're so uptight about. I mean here you've got this terrific chance to get out of this crummy town and this crummy school and go someplace neat for a while, and you're acting like they're sending you off to some egg salad plant where all you'll get to do for the next seven or eight months is peel hard-boileds."

"What brought eggs to mind?"

"Well, isn't peeling eggs the thing everybody hates to do the most in the world?"

"I don't know. I haven't got around to asking everybody."

It was Saturday, and Lucy was spending the night. They were up in Kate's room changing into their pajamas before going downstairs to watch *The Ghoul Show* on TV. That night it was "The Mummy's Revenge," which was one of Lucy's favorites.

"What makes you think this move is going to be so neat?" Kate asked.

"I don't know. Any place has got to be neater than Springville."

"You say that because you haven't been anywhere else. You know what Port Williams is? It's Springville, only on a river. It's just as small and dull as here. I guess it's better than if I had to go to New York. That would be really scary. I'm sure everybody there talks faster and dresses better and knows more than I do. Or California, where all the kids are probably so cool, you wouldn't stand a chance if you were from the Midwest and not blond and didn't know how to surf."

"So what's the problem? You sort of know what it's like there, and it's sort of like here, but it's not here. Sounds like a perfect combination to me."

"You're missing the point. It's not Port Williams that's the problem. It's my Aunt Caroline."

"You think she's going to beat you up and stuff you in the closet and feed you bowls of gruel like they always do to the poor visiting cousin in all those old English books?"

"Not quite. I mean the way Aunt Caroline is awful is a little more subtle than that."

"Like?"

"Well, she's sort of the hale and hearty type. Real interested in what you're doing. And she's always got a brilliant idea for some terrific fun you could be having. Two summers ago we spent a week there, and one night it just came to her in a flash that instead of hanging around their house, we could all be out camping. When we got up the next morning, she had the sleeping bags and knapsacks all packed into the back of their station wagon, and off we went for two days."

"Was it fun?"

"Well, sort of. For me anyway. We saw two bears one morning. But can you imagine my mother camping?"

"I get this picture of her trying to vacuum the leaves off the ground because they're so messy."

"She held herself back, but I think something like that was in the back of her mind most of the time."

"Old Aunt Caroline doesn't sound all that bad. So she's a little enthusiastic."

"I didn't mean to make her out to be a horror. It's just that we don't match up too well. I mostly like to be left alone and if there's one thing she isn't, it's a leaver-alone."

"Does an Uncle Somebody come with Aunt Caroline?"

"Frank. He's okay. I still haven't told you the worst part, though. It's my cousin Laura. She's a year older than us. I absolutely detest her. She's worse, if possible, than Stacy Adams."

24

"Oh," Lucy said, "I wouldn't worry about that too much. She'll probably practice her clarinet down at school most of the time and you won't hardly ever have to listen to her."

"Lucy, sometimes you are thicker than a Bombay Elm."

"What?"

"Come on. Let's go down and turn on the movie."

"Oh, I forgot. We'd better hurry. I don't want you to miss the part after the archaeologists leave the tomb for the night — they've just discovered the mummy and taken the lid off his box — and the mummy starts mooooo-ving oh sooooo slooooowly like this."

"Lucy! Stop it. I'm going to be too scared to watch."

"You'll be okay. We'll keep the lights on and you can check the door locks during commercials."

The next month flew by. The last two weeks before Christmas vacation were always a breeze. The teachers were in a jolly mood, and the normal routine was thrown into wonderful chaos by all the holiday plays and pageants and parties that the school let the kids get away with. The two weeks of Christmas break were a blur of present-buying and tree-trimming and cookie-baking and relative-visiting. Kate was grateful for all the activity. It kept her from stopping long enough to think. Thinking was a sad business these days. She couldn't help focusing in on the day after New Year's, which was sure to be the end of any fun for the next seven or eight months.

And so when January 2 finally arrived, Kate found herself all packed and yet totally unprepared. Her mother (trying to put a happy face on things, Kate suspected) had been just brimming over with good spirits all morning. She had fixed Kate's favorite breakfast — pancakes and bacon. The condemned man's last meal. She wasn't about to be bought off so easily. As many ways as she had tried to figure it, she always came back to her first gut reaction — that her parents were doing a really crummy thing to her.

At first, she had retaliated by pouting, but after a few days it became apparent that all her sulking wasn't going to budge them one inch, and was for sure going to get her grounded if she kept it up much longer. Then she had tried to reason with them. She told them how uncomfortable and out of it she was going to feel living in a strange house full of distant relatives. This was about as effective as the pouting.

They were very nice and very calm, but couldn't see any other way. They couldn't leave her home alone, and her grandmother was too old to take care of her. None of the Springville relatives had room. For a couple of days, there was a brief glimmer of hope. Lucy talked things over with her mother, who thought it would be fine if Kate came to stay with them. It meant bunking in with Lucy and her French horn and her piles of sheet music and her steady stream of boy craziness, but that seemed like small stuff compared to moving to Aunt Caroline's. She could barely wait to get home from school that day to tell her mother that she had found a way out that would make everybody happy. And she was crushed when her mother dismissed the notion out of hand.

"It's completely unthinkable," was what she had said.

"But why?" Kate had asked.

"Don't question my judgement, Kate. You're just going to have to trust that I know what's best for you."

Kate thought some more about it that night in bed and figured that it probably had something to do with the fact that Lucy's parents were drunk an awful lot of the time. She thought about explaining to her mother that that hardly mattered at all to her and Lucy, but decided that it probably wouldn't do any good.

And so, despite all her efforts and thinking and rethinking, there she stood out at the airport in front of Gate 2, where in ten minutes she would get on the plane to Chicago, where she would catch the short flight to Port Williams. It wasn't a terrific send-off. She was crushed that they were doing this to her. They were disappointed at how badly she had been behaving about it. And to top things off they were nervous and determined, it seemed, to cram these last ten minutes with a crash course on life.

"Got your ticket?"

"If you go to the bathroom on the plane, be sure to take your purse with you."

"Don't forget to give Aunt Caroline the candy."

"Make sure to offer to do your share of the chores."

"Don't take seconds unless they're offered."

"And if it's liver, don't let on that you don't like it."

"Don't be inviting your friends over all the time. Remember you're only a guest yourself." (Fat chance she'd have any friends to worry about inviting over, Kate thought.)

When they got down to "Don't forget to

brush your teeth in the morning *and* at night," Kate told them she thought she'd better get on the plane before it took off without her.

As it came to final good-byes, Kate grew uneasy. She didn't want to go and knew they weren't all that happy about letting her go. Still, they *were* shoving her off, and there was a part of her that didn't want to let them see how much it hurt. In the end, she let her dad give her one of his bone-crushing hugs. After all, he couldn't really help being sent to the edges of the earth by his company. With her mother, though, she backed off after a quick kiss on the cheek. If she had really wanted to, her mother could have probably talked Daddy into letting her stay at home with Kate. But she hadn't.

The trip itself was sort of fun. Kate had never gone anywhere by herself, and she liked the grown-up feeling it gave her. She strapped herself in, watched the take-off out the window, took a Coke and a little foil-wrapped package of nuts from the stewardess when she came around, and wrote a postcard to Lucy. "Dropping you a line from 30,000 feet" was all she could think of to say, which was corny, but Lucy would probably like it. In the pocket in front of her, she found an airlines magazine with a story in it on Tucson, which looked like a pretty nifty place. Much niftier, at any rate, than Port Williams.

She had a two-hour layover in Chicago. She took part of the traveling money her dad had given her and bought three candy bars and two magazines — one on teenage fashions and another called *Your Hairdo*, then found a place to sit in a long row of black plastic waiting chairs. Next to her was a middle-aged woman with a daughter about Kate's age and two small boys. After a while, they got to talking. They were all on their way to Missouri to meet the woman's husband. He was a career Army officer and had just been transferred to a base there. Kate told them she was going to Tucson to ride in the Junior Rodeo. She didn't know if they believed her. Later, on the plane, she wondered why she had done it.

She spent most of the second flight dreading the meeting with Aunt Caroline and Uncle Frank, who would probably be out at the arrival gate with banners and a full band, or something equally outrageous and embarrassing. At the very least, they would be all over her like a human Welcome Wagon, making her the center of the spectacle they were creating.

What actually happened was the only

terrible thing Kate hadn't imagined in advance. No one was there. Well, several people were there, but they weren't anybody she knew, and in ten minutes or so, they had all wandered off with other people from her plane, leaving her more alone than she had ever felt in her life.

They're probably just stuck in traffic, or having trouble finding a place to park, she told herself, and sat down to wait with her magazines. When she had looked at all the outfits three times and all the hairdos twice and even read the back-pages ads for blackhead removers and while-you-sleep Spanish lessons, she looked up at the wall clock and saw that an hour had passed. Something was definitely wrong. Maybe this was Aunt Caroline's subtle way of showing that she didn't really want Kate at all. Maybe if she called, Aunt Caroline would just say "Kate who?" But calling did seem like the only thing to do. She couldn't very well spend the next seven months in the airport, and if she called her parents long distance, they would just tell her to call Aunt Caroline. And so she dug the slip of paper out of her purse, went over to the pay phone, dialed the number, let it ring five times and was just about to hang up when a breathless Aunt Caroline answered.

"Hi, Aunt Caroline. It's me. Kate."

"Katie dear! How are you?"

"Just fine."

"You know, I was just telling Frank this morning how much fun I think it's going to be having you here."

"I'm looking forward to it too."

"You know, we certainly have a terrific connection. It almost sounds like you're right here."

"Well, I am sort of."

"How do you mean?"

"Well, I'm at the airport."

"Here? In Port Williams?"

"Yes."

"Do your parents know?"

"Well, yes. They put me on the plane this morning."

"You mean you're supposed to be here? Today's the day?"

"I think so. I mean, well I'm here and this is the day we thought I was supposed to come."

"Just a second. I'll go check." Kate waited through a lot of paper shuffling and crackling sounds. "Well, right you are. Here's your mother's letter and right here in the third paragraph it says January 2. Somehow I had it in mind that you were coming in on Friday. Now where did I ever get that idea?"

"I could go back and come in then."

"Of course not. You just wait right there. We're painting the laundry room today, but as soon as I clean up and change, I'll be right out there to get you. Wait by the front door. Don't just take a ride out here with a stranger or anything."

"I wasn't thinking of that."

"No, I don't suppose you would be. Okay. See you in a little while."

Kate only had to wait fifteen minutes or so before Aunt Caroline's battered old station wagon pulled up. Apparently she had decided to save time by not changing, as she was still wearing a pair of spattered jeans and an old workshirt and one of those paper caps they give out at paint stores. The hat made Aunt Caroline — who already had short hair that looked like it had a direct current running through it — look even more comic than usual.

"Hop in, Katie. Just toss those bags in the back seat."

"It's good to see you again, Aunt Caroline."

"Good to see you. You look so smart and grown-up in that suit."

"My mom bought it for the trip."

"I don't think you'll get much wear out of it here. I had trouble getting Laura to wear a skirt to poor Uncle Albert's funeral."

33

"How is Laura these days?"

"Don't ask me. I'm the last to know. She's been wearing a wedding band lately. I thought maybe she'd gotten married and forgotten to tell us, but then I figured if she was married, she probably would have moved out. Last week I overheard one of her friends asking her if she liked going steady, so I guess that's what's going on."

"Don't you know who the guy is?"

"Well, now that you mention it, the crew does seem to have whittled down to a tall, skinny fellow. A Bob, I think."

"I guess Laura's pretty busy most of the time."

"Hardly ever see her. And now, of course, she has the job after school at the cleaners."

"Does she like it?"

"She likes the money. She hates having to pull things out of strange people's pockets."

"Why does she have to do that?"

"Well, they have to check things before they run them through. You wouldn't want to put a sport coat in the machine with a candy bar in it."

"Oh, I see."

"Maybe she can get you a job there too. Give you some extra spending money."

"I don't know. I've never had a job before."

34

"I don't think they're too fussy about credentials at the cleaners. Well, here we are."

Aunt Caroline's house was both better and worse than Kate's. It was bigger, and had bigger yards in the front and back. But it was a little ramshackle with paint peeling off the siding, and a big sag in the wooden front porch. Kate could remember when they had bought the place. Aunt Caroline had written Kate's mother that they had found this terrific place on the outskirts of town, just before you got out into farmland, and how it was really a beautiful old place, but needed a little renovating, which they thought they could do within a year or so. That was five years ago and, driving up to it, Kate thought it looked a little worse, if possible, than the other two times she had seen it. But then in the mood she was in she probably would have been able to find fault with the Taj Mahal.

"Here," Aunt Caroline said as they got out of the car, "let me help you with those bags. We were going to put you in with Laura, but then thought you might like a little privacy, so we moved a few things up into the attic. It's a little rustic, but I think it'll do fine."

They came in through the back door, went through the kitchen into the back hall, then up a flight of narrow wood stairs.

"Be careful here," Aunt Caroline warned Kate. "The third step is missing. I was meaning to fix it before you got here, but you got the jump on me. Just remember it's the third one from the bottom when you come down in the dark at night."

One thing Kate had to admit about the attic was that it was the biggest room she was ever likely to sleep in. Even after they got past the part that was filled with boxes and old lamps and a three-legged chair and tied-together stacks of old magazines, there was still at least half of it left over for what had been designated as her room. The old iron bed, and sit-down vanity with mirror, and chest of drawers, and desk, and old overstuffed chair that Aunt Caroline had arranged at the far end by the single window barely took up a quarter of the space.

"Is this all you brought?" Aunt Caroline asked her.

"No. Daddy sent a couple of trunks by Railway Express. They're supposed to be here by the end of the week."

"Well, why don't you unpack what you've got here. You know, get yourself settled, then come on down and we'll see if we can dig up a snack for you. If you've got some old clothes, put them on and you can help me and Frank finish up the painting."

"Okay."

Aunt Caroline was halfway down the stairs when she yelled up, "And don't worry about bats."

Kate didn't want to ask whether she shouldn't worry because there weren't any, or because there were so many that it wouldn't do any good to worry about them.

She started to unpack, then gave up, laid down on the bed and cried half an hour's worth of hopeless, silent tears.

Chapter 3

A AUNT Caroline's two weeks though, this fear of... was... you about.

Ever since she had found out that she was going to have to come to Port Williams, Kate had been dreading it. But it had mostly been a dread of the unknown, of living in a strange place full of strangers, or, in reverse, of not being where things and people — whether she liked them or not — were at least familiar to her.

By the time she had been at Aunt Caroline's two weeks, though, this fear of the unknown had disappeared completely. Now she woke up every morning with a dread of the known. This included just about everything about life at Aunt Caroline's, which was the opposite in nearly every way of life in her own house.

From the minute they got up in the morning, everything in the Meyers' house was total chaos. Kate was used to her mother getting up early and fixing breakfast while Kate and her dad took their regular turns in the bathroom. At the Meyers', no one got out of bed a minute before they absolutely had to, which got everyone to the bathroom at about the same time. The accepted way to get your turn was to pound on the door and harrass the person inside into coming out. Since Kate couldn't imagine taunting Uncle Frank the way Laura and Aunt Caroline did, by asking him if he had fallen asleep in there, she wound up brushing her teeth at the kitchen sink the first three mornings. Then she figured out that, by getting up fifteen minutes earlier, she could avoid the rush entirely, go back to her room for a while, and leave the battlefield to the rest of them.

Breakfast wasn't so much a distinct meal as it was an instant replay of dinner. Everyone just poked through the refrigerator and took whatever leftovers looked interesting, and the kinds of things that looked interesting and appetizing to them at 7:30 in the morning were a continual source of amazement to Kate. It made her go a little green at the gills just to watch Uncle Frank down a bowl of sauerkraut and ham hocks while Laura polished off what was left of the cauliflower with cheese sauce. And so, as politely as possible, she turned down their offers of cold pot roast or brussel sprouts and stuck to bread and jam. She was looking forward to a switch to toast and jam when Aunt Caroline got around to fixing the toaster. (Any day now, she had been assured.)

After this stand-up meal, everyone made a simultaneous mad-dash exit. Uncle Frank took the car to the plant. Aunt Caroline ran out to join the car pool of other teachers who usually had been honking outside for ten minutes or so. Kate and Laura walked together the five blocks to Port Williams High School.

Laura was about as pukey as Kate remembered her. She had come home about an hour after Kate had arrived that first day, and managed, within ten minues, to make Kate sorry for the second time that day that she had ever let her mother buy her the sensible tweed traveling suit she had worn on the flight.

"I almost didn't recognize you so dressed up, Kate," she said. "Is that what they're wearing in Springville this year?" It was just the kind of smirky put-down she would have expected from Stacy Adams.

"Not really. My mother made me get it. She thinks people ought to dress up for trips." Kate wasn't too proud about making her mother the fall guy, but it seemed the only way out.

"So how are things in Springville? I met this guy from there when I went to the homecoming weekend at State, and he said the kids there are really wild. Tom Brandt. Do you know him?"

"I don't think so. I don't know too many

older guys. Maybe it's the seniors he was talking about. The juniors I know are pretty tame." She didn't think it was necessary to mention that all the juniors she really knew were Lucy, who was still about as tame as she had been in sixth grade.

"It's the same around here. Sometimes it's so dull, I could just die. I can't wait until next year when I can go away to college. That's where everything's happening."

"Where are you going to go?"

"I'm not sure. I'm having a little trouble making up my mind."

"But don't you have to have applied by now to get in next fall?"

"Some of the kids have already gotten accepted somewhere, but I want to hang loose about it for a while. Look around, you know. Maybe I won't even go right away. I'm thinking of maybe working a year first."

"But I thought you were dying to get away."

"Yeah, well. Hey, you know it's great having you here, Kate. I'll have to show you around, you know, introduce you to some of the kids sometime. Next week maybe. I've really been frazzled lately with working and the Christmas play and all. Mom, could you make me a sandwich or something while I change? I'm supposed to be

41

over at Mimi's in half an hour. The guys are coming by there to pick us up for the sleigh ride. If you're still up when I get in, Kate, I'll probably see you then. It's really great having you. Or did I already say that. See, I *am* getting flaky."

Laura never did come through on her promise to show Kate around. Kate couldn't really blame her. Laura hung around with the cool crowd of seniors and Kate couldn't really imagine that they would be thrilled to have Laura's out-of-it, year-younger cousin from Springville tagging along. She just wouldn't fit in. Laura must have seen this in advance. And actually, Kate was sort of grateful for Laura's neglect. If she had tried to wedge Kate into her circle of friends, it would have only been an embarrassment for both of them.

On the whole, Kate thought the best she could expect from the next few months was being ignored. At school, at least, her wish was being granted. Back in Springville, a transfer student was a big event. Almost everybody at Benton had known each other practically since first grade, and any new kid got inspected, and talked about, and usually made fun of if anything about him was the slightest bit different from the way Springville kids dressed, talked, or acted. At least Port Williams wasn't so dumb in that way. Kate guessed it was probably because of the plant. It was the plant that had brought Uncle Frank and lots of other people to Port Williams, and was still bringing them in and transferring them out. So Kate guessed that new kids coming or old ones leaving just wasn't much of a big deal around there.

A few kids in her classes had come up and talked to her the first day after Christmas break, but after that no one paid her much attention. Which was a relief at first — not to be the object of curious stares and the subject of whispered conversations. It left her free to go along by herself, unbothered, through the measured routine of school days. The hard mornings of homeroom, English, history, and geometry. The easy afternoons of lunch, study hall, gym, Spanish, and biology. If anyone did notice her, they might just think she was aloof.

Back home, she had grown used to not being noticed much, and to settling for friends who were as out of the social mainstream as she was. At first she didn't understand why the loneliness bothered her so much more in Port Williams. After a couple of weeks, she figured out that it was probably because, underneath her despair, she had secretly been hoping things would be different here.

She started thinking of ways she could make friends with some of the kids who interested her. The problem was that she couldn't think of any reason they would be interested in *her*. And so she scaled down to trying to make friends with Florence Brock, who, because of their last names — Brock and Brown — sat in front of Kate in both English and geometry, where the teachers assigned seats alphabetically. Florence Brock looked like someone who couldn't possibly be overloaded with friends. In addition to her thick glasses, and terrible pimples, and perpetual odor of blouses worn a day too long, she was the one in both classes who always knew the answer, and always raised her hand to show she knew the answer — a practice that didn't win her any popularity contests. But she was smart, and Kate suspected that the reason she never talked to any of the other kids might just be that she was shy. Sort of like Kate. And so, after a few false starts, Kate finally screwed up her courage and asked Florence, at the start of one geometry class, if she could borrow a pencil. Florence Brock didn't even turn around. At first Kate thought maybe she hadn't heard. She was about to try again when Florence passed back half of an un-sharpened beauty she must have had in the bottom of her pencil case since freshman year. Wrapped around it, secured with a rubber band, was a note. Kate opened it and read: "Let's not make a habit of this, okay?"

Well, so much for a heavyweight friendship with Florence Brock, Kate thought, and tried to slough it off. But the sting lasted for days. It was the double indignity of being snubbed by someone who got snubbed by everyone else.

Worse still was what she was going through at home. Within a week after Kate's arrival, Aunt Caroline started an off-and-on campaign to shape her up. New clothes were Point One.

"Have you got a minute?" was how Aunt Caroline approached the subject one afternoon when Kate came in from school.

"Sure."

"I've been thinking about the way you dress."

"You don't like my clothes."

"Well, they're certainly well made and sensible and look like they'll give you a lot of wear and all that. And they're always neat and pressed and clean. I was just thinking that they might be a little, well, a little middle-aged. I mean take what you've got on right now. I think a pretty, sixteen-year-old girl could afford to go a little brighter. Brown skirt, gray blouse, black sweater. Well, it's more what you'd expect on someone more serious and severe and older. One of those women professors who

45

specialize in Egyptology and spend their Saturdays at lectures on the discovery of a new sarcophagus."

"What's a sarcophagus?"

"Like a coffin, only stone."

"Oh."

"I'm not being critical, you understand. Just trying to help."

"Sure."

And so the plan was for Laura to set it up for Kate to work Saturdays at the cleaners. Then in a month or two, when Kate had enough saved up, she could go along with her aunt and Laura on one of their shopping trips to Chicago.

Actually, this part of Aunt Caroline's plan was sort of okay by Kate. She didn't mind the idea of working at the cleaners if Laura could pave the way for her. It wasn't as if she had anything terrific to do on Saturdays anyway. And she would like to get some new clothes. Stuff she'd pick out herself. She hadn't even been too offended that Aunt Caroline thought what she wore was drab. So did Kate when she let herself think about it, which wasn't often. Mostly they were things her mother had bought or made for her, and she had gone along with. So Kate had pretty much given up on the idea of dressing the way she liked, and talked herself into thinking that it just didn't matter that much one way or the other. Now that it looked like Aunt Caroline was going to let her buy her own things, she started buying fashion magazines regularly, and watched carefully what the sharp girls were wearing around school.

Point Two of Aunt Caroline's plan was the creepy part. It was interests. Aunt Caroline didn't think Kate had enough of them. And so now Kate spent her Tuesday nights with Aunt Caroline at her découpage class down at the Y, laminating travel photos onto the top of a wooden jewelry box. Kate didn't have the nerve to tell Aunt Caroline that she hated découpage, that she thought all the purses and jewelry boxes and picture frames everyone in the class was working on looked better plain than they were going to look with pictures laminated on top of them. Now she was thinking that she should have spoken up and asserted herself a little in the beginning. She could take the découpaging, but now that Aunt Caroline misguidedly thought that Kate was thrilled at having this one new interest, she had, with considerable effort, managed to get Kate into her Thursday night karate class.

Kate supposed she could get out of it by telling Aunt Caroline that going down to the junior high gym every week for three hours to grunt and chop away at housewives in Chinese jackets was not really her idea of a big thrill. But she was afraid that backing away from any of Aunt Caroline's schemes would make the Meyers think she was even duller and more uptight than they already so obviously thought she was.

She wasn't sure why she cared what the Meyers thought of her, considering that she thought they were at least a little lunatic. If she were a keeper in a booby hatch, she wouldn't care that all the people who thought they were Napoleon thought she was nuts for not thinking she was Napoleon.

And it wasn't that their enthusiasms were so contagious. At any rate, she hadn't caught any of them so far. But most of their eccentricities were the free-spirited, zest-for-life kind, and if you shrank away from them out of caution or even just good sense it made you come off as a wet blanket.

Like last week Uncle Frank had been cleaning out the front hall closet and discovered that their sleeping bags were "guaranteed comfortable in Arctic temperatures." Aunt Caroline thought this warranted an immediate consumer test. And so that night, after turning down Uncle Frank's offer of their extra bag, Kate stayed alone in the house while the three of them slept out on the snow-covered patio. Lying up in her attic room, listening to them in the yard below her window, toasting marshmallows over the grill and singing "Ragtime Cowboy Joe," Kate knew they were disappointed in her for not joining in. And in spite of thinking they were nuts for spending the night out in thirty-degree temperatures, she was a little disappointed in herself. But she wasn't quite sure why. It was befuddling.

It wasn't that they were trying to make her feel bad. She knew that. Actually, they could hardly be nicer. They always tried to include her, and when she declined they usually let it go. She guessed it was the way they did it that bothered her. The way they acted sort of sad, but resigned. As if when it came to having fun, she was hopelessly retarded.

Worse than this, though, was when Aunt Caroline did put on the pressure, like with the découpage and the karate. And worse than Aunt Caroline's concerned enforcement was Laura's enforced concern. Kate had been told enough times by her parents to "be nice to so-and-so," that she could see clearly that Laura was under instructions to be nice to her.

And so most of their contact, aside from dinner and the walk to school, came down to the few times a week Laura made sure, within earshot of her parents, to spend five minutes or so "being nice" to Kate.

"How's it going, Katie?" was the standard opener. This time Kate was in the kitchen polishing her shoes and Laura was making one of her five-minute pit stops between activities.

"Okay."

"I see you've got Emily Dickinson there. That must mean you've got old Hinckleshmidt for English. Old Hinkydink just loves Emily Dickinson. You'll probably be doing Dickinson for the rest of the year."

"Oh, she's not so bad."

"You've got to be kidding. No one in the whole school can stand her."

"Oh, Miss Hinckleshmidt. You're right. She is sort of boring. And she's real tough, especially on the boys. I meant Emily Dickinson. I sort of like her."

"I guess she's okay, if you like poetry. I just get bored with all that beating around the bush. Sometimes I just wish they'd spit it out and get it over with."

"You might like some of the modern poets better. I've got some books I could lend you."

"Like I have time to read for fun with all the stuff they load us up with at school. I guess you probably read a lot," Laura said, in the same tone of voice someone would use if they were saying, "I suppose you like to wear your shoes on your ears."

"Yeah, well, I've got the time. The classes here aren't as much work as they are in Springville. Maybe that's just the junior classes, though. It sounds like you've got it worse."

"I guess it's that I don't really have time for school. They already keep us there until 3:30 every day. When do they expect us to do homework too? I'm at the cleaners until 7:00 on Tuesday and Thursday. Last semester I had play practice three nights a week, and it looks like I'm going to get a part in this new one. And weekends, forget it. I mean, if you've got any kind of social life at all. Oh well, you can imagine."

"Yeah, I can imagine."

"Hey. Maybe you want to double sometime."

"With who?"

"Me and Bob. He could fix you up with someone. One of the guys on the basketball team."

"Oh, that's okay. Thanks anyway."

Watching Laura's reaction, Kate realized that until that moment she had only come across "heave a sigh of relief" as a figure of speech and hadn't actually seen anyone do it.

"Do you date much? I don't mean here. I know you haven't had much of a chance to meet anyone yet. But back home?"

"Well, my folks haven't really let me start dating yet," Kate said. That little white lie again.

"Really? I can't believe it. I mean, I knew they were strict, but you're sixteen, for crying out loud. You don't have to worry about that around here, if that's what you were thinking. Mom doesn't care if you go out, as long as it's not on motorcycles." Laura lowered her voice so that Aunt Caroline, who was doing her Royal Canadian Air Force exercises in the next room, wouldn't hear. "That's the only thing she's funny about. She thinks as soon as you get on a motorcycle, you're heading off for Dead Man's Curve or something and that'll be the end of you. So if you're into that sort of thing, have the guys pick you up down the street or something."

"I'm not into motorcycles."

"The other thing is that she just loves it when I have kids down to the rec room. You know, to play records and stuff. So I'm sure she wouldn't mind if you did. We can ask her."

"That's okay. I'll just wait until it comes up. I mean right now there isn't really anyone I'd want to have over anyway."

"Yeah, well I'd better get going. I'm supposed to meet Bob when he gets out of basketball practice."

"I ran into him in the front hall the other night when he came by to get you. He's cute."

"You think so?"

"Really."

"I guess he'll do. Well, I'd better let you get upstairs and start cracking those books. Maybe when you're finished with your homework, you could do mine for me."

"Oh sure," Kate said, and laughed to show she knew it was just friendly teasing.

Of course, she really knew it was nothing of the kind. Friendly teasing is what you do with someone you like and consider an equal. Nor was it a vicious snipe. That's what you do to someone you don't like, but consider a threat. What this was — and it pretty much summed up the way Laura always talked to Kate — was a thoughtless, offhand dismissal of someone who just doesn't matter.

After two weeks in Port Williams, this sickening realization was unavoidable. To Uncle Frank, she was the new person who said, "Please pass the salt" at dinner. To Aunt Caroline, she was this week's piece of bland raw material, an undécoupaged purse that might make a briefly amusing project. To Laura, she was the relative to "be nice to" in very free moments. To the kids in school, she was simply nonexistent.

At home, with her parents and Lucy and the other girls around, she had been able to fool herself. Here, though, it was all too clear that in sixteen years all she had become was someone who didn't matter. She had never been so lonely. Before, she could at least go off by herself. Lately, though, when she was alone, she found she didn't much like the company.

It was a hard one to see a way out of. She thought about making herself over into the kind of person who counted. The new Kate she had in mind had the coolest guys in school calling to ask her out and the rest settling for just being around her — wanting her to go for rides in their new cars, getting her to play volleyball with them on Saturday afternoon, kidding around with her by the lockers — just because she was so much fun to be with. The other girls would be envious, of course, but never catty because she was such a good friend to all of them, and a terrific source of advice on clothes and dating.

The one small problem was that she had no idea of how to get to be this kind of person. She didn't even know where to start. Finally, she decided the first step was to go down to the drugstore and buy a tube of Summer Peach Frosted Lip Gloss and a small bottle of "Devastating" cologne —

the two most sure-fire items advertised in this month's magazines. But once she had put them on up in her room that night, she was at a complete loss for where to go from there.

Most of her worries lately had focused on the long seven months ahead. At that moment though, as she sat down on her bed, it seemed like her whole life was going to be a long, tough thing to get through.

Chapter 4

It was late Tuesday night — close to midnight. Kate thought everyone had gone to sleep. She was sitting on her bed, a mirror propped on her knees, trying to highlight her cheeks with blusher according to the diagram in the magazine lying open next to her. By the time she heard the thud of someone leaping over the missing third step, it was too late to fold everything up, turn out the light, and pretend she was asleep. She was immobilized with the horror of being discovered in the midst of this idiotic activity. She sat frozen, hoping it wasn't her aunt.

It was Laura.

"Hi," she said from the top of the stairs across the attic from Kate. "You know, with all this dark, empty space, and you way off in the distance in a room that's not really a room — it's kind of like a movie set-up."

"I hadn't thought of it that way," Kate said, trying not to sound nervous while at the same time being very nervous that Laura would come any closer.

"Does it ever give you the creeps up here?"

"Not any more. At first it did a little. You have to get used to the bats."

"There aren't really any, are there?"

"Not yet. If they ever found out about this place, they'd love it, though, don't you think?"

"For sure. Hey, I'm glad you're still up. I was trying to be real quiet in case you were already asleep. I've got to have this dumb paper done for English by tomorrow and I've messed it up so many times that I've run out of looseleaf paper. I thought you might have a few sheets I could borrow."

"Sure. I've got a whole extra pack you can have. I'll get it for you," Kate said, hoping to keep Laura at bay by the stairway. But she was already bounding across the attic.

"Hey, you're a lifesaver. I can get it myself, though. Just tell me where it is." She stopped short in the middle of Kate's room. "Do you always put on make-up before you go to bed?"

"Oh, I'm just, you know, sort of practicing." Kate hated it when she could hear herself sounding so nervous and defensive.

"I didn't know you even wore make-up."

"Well, I don't really yet. So far I'm just, you know, like I said, practicing."

"Practicing what?" Laura asked. Kate couldn't tell whether she was really curious or just baiting her.

"Oh, getting it on right and stuff like that. It's this article — it's a dumb article — about how to make your cheekbones more prominent."

"Oh."

"It's just something to do. Something to fool around with. I guess it sounds dumb."

"No. Well, a little, I guess. Not the practicing part, but the not wearing it out once you've got it on. But I guess even that's not so dumb. I've had at least three hairdos that went straight from the rollers to the shower. And when I was in junior high, some creepy boy told me I walked funny. For a while after that I practiced walking in front of the mirror. Trying out different ways. That was about the same time I worked on changing my handwriting into something with more flair. I was calling myself Lauri then. With an 'i.' When I signed it, I dotted the 'i' with a little heart. Mom saw it that way once on a thank-you note I was sending to Aunt Edna and said it was the stupidest thing she had ever seen. I guess she embarrassed me out of it. I know I went back to using Laura pretty soon after that. So I guess everyone practices and experiments with different stuff. I seem to do it less than I used to, but I don't know if anyone ever gets so satisfied that they quit entirely. Like Dad. Last year he grew the worst mustache in the world. It wasn't until everyone told him he looked like a cheap detective that he finally shaved it off."

"I really am getting pretty close to wearing make-up outside, I think," Kate said. "I figure while I'm here would probably be a good time to try it out. I mean I don't think your mom would care too much. That was part of the problem at home. My mother would've gone through the roof."

"I don't think Mom would care if we wore fake Dracula fangs. The only thing that gets her is pierced ears. She thinks they're primitive. I even had my hair bleached platinum once and it didn't get a rise out of her. I was sort of hoping it would."

"Why?"

"Well then I could have gotten rid of it, you know, told everyone my mother put the squelch on it. As it was I had to go around looking stupid for a month or so because I was too proud to admit what a giant mistake it had been."

"What happened after a month?"

"Oh, I just told everybody it didn't seem

worth all the upkeep and had it dyed back to my real color. I think there's still about an inch of platinum under here somewhere."

"Your own hair's so nice. Why'd you ever do it in the first place?"

"Oh, I'd seen this old movie on TV. I thought I'd look like Marilyn Monroe, but it came out more Mae West."

"Maybe I shouldn't try the make-up."

"I don't see why not. That blusher looks good. Real natural."

"Oh, this isn't all of it. I've got lots more in the box there."

"Can I look?"

"Sure."

"Oh, you really do have a lot. There must be fifty dollars worth of stuff in here. And none of it has seen the light of day? Gee, I think you ought to start wearing it just to get back some of your investment. You know, this is really sort of a surprise. I didn't think you ever did anything that wasn't serious."

"How do you mean?"

"I don't know," Laura said, pulling Kate's desk chair up to the bed and sitting down. "It's just hard to imagine you doing anything silly. You seem like the kind of person who thinks a lot of large thoughts about life."

"Who could think large thoughts all the time?"

"Well, if you had to think about something small, you'd probably think about it practically. Like if you went out to buy a sweater, I can't imagine you picking one because it was dynamite looking. I'd think you'd look for how much wear it would give you and how likely it was to get pills on the elbows. That sort of thing."

"It's worse than I thought."

"What?"

"Do I really come off that dull?"

"I wouldn't say dull. Sensible."

"That's worse."

"Come on. There are times I'd give anything to be more like you. Sensible. Organized. Self-sufficient. I'm always at such loose ends. I'm always down to my last pair of socks before I remember to toss my laundry down the chute. And I'm always getting graded down for being late with papers I forgot had even been assigned. And I don't ever feel like I have very much inside me to fall back on. I've got to have lots of people around and lots happening all the time, or I get terrifically bored. I really envy the way you seem to enjoy being by yourself so much of the time. I mean I figured you were a person with a lot of interesting stuff going on inside. See, you can afford to be stuck-up. If I told everybody to fly a kite, I'd be all alone. Two weeks of that and I'd die of boredom."

"Is that what you think? That I'm stuck-up?"

"I didn't mean it as an insult."

"You didn't ever think it might just be that I was a social moron?"

Laura got up off the chair, pulled one of the pillows from under the bedspread, and propped herself up with it against the footboard so that she was stretched out on the bed facing Kate.

"You don't mind, do you? Mother must've got that chair when they auctioned off the remains of a torture chamber."

"It isn't very comfortable, is it?"

"You study on it every night?"

"I don't really study all that much," Kate said.

"Is that what you think?"

"That I don't study all that much?"

"That you're a social moron."

"A lot of the time."

"You could've fooled me."

"Really?"

"But then I'm easy to fool. I take most things at face value. I'm nearly always wrong."

"And my face value is that I'm so cool I don't need anybody else around?"

"Not exactly. It was more that I figured

you for one of those people who doesn't care if she's a little out of it. After all, being in it isn't all that terrific."

"It looks pretty terrific to me," Kate said, idly fingering the pages of her magazine rather than looking straight across the bed at Laura.

"Oh, well, it's not nothing, of course. Like with Bob. Part of it is that I really like him. That we really get along — most of the time, anyway — and have a good time together and all that. But another part of it is knowing that practically every girl in school would like to have him if they could. Being in the sorority is the same sort of thing."

"I didn't know you were in a sorority," Kate said.

"They're not allowed. At school we wear our pins inside our blouses. The next time you're in the john or the gym or someplace where you'd run into seniors, just look close. Anytime you see a girl with a little gold straight pin come through on the left side of her blouse, you'll know. Anyway, part of what's nice about belonging is that they're all my friends and I really like them. But it's also that they're all the best girls in the class. Either they're the best looking, or they're cheerleaders, or they're the funniest. When you're in the sorority, you go to the best parties and hang around

63

with the coolest guys, and you don't have to be bothered with the twinkies."

"Like me."

"No, you don't even fit into the picture. You've just dropped in for a few months and decided to sit this one out, which seems like a reasonable way to handle it, I guess."

"What if I decided I didn't want to sit it out?"

"You mean what if you wanted to get into things?"

"Yeah."

"I suppose you could do it. It might be tough at first. New kids have it rougher. Unless they're obviously stars of some sort. Like Coleen Quinn. Everybody knew when she moved here that she'd already been on the Olympic skating team and spent a summer with the Ice Follies. The first day of classes kids were practically asking for her autograph in the halls. You haven't been in the Olympics, have you, and forgot to tell me about it?"

"Not that I remember."

"Then it'll be tougher. We could say you're from Hollywood and are cozy with a lot of movie stars."

"I'm a terrible liar," Kate told her, then told her about the lie she had told at the airport in Chicago.

"Junior Rodeo! That's the dinkiest lie I've ever heard. That's really pitiful, Kate."

"Well, you see what I mean. I don't think lying is the answer for me."

"Okay. Let me think about it. We can probably come up with a fast way to slip you in. I'd better get back to this paper. It looks like it's going to be an all-nighter."

"What's it on?"

"Mark Twain."

"He's pretty easy. I mean there's lots of stuff you can say about him."

"Not if you're only on Page 42 of *Tom Sawyer* and just read the Classic Comics version of *Huckleberry Finn*."

"I could help you. We did him last year in Springville."

"Thanks anyway, Katie, but I don't think it'd work. The whole thing's just hopeless. I got an F from her last semester. The best I ever did on a paper for her was a C— and she told me after class that she had graded me up for 'neatness of presentation.' That sounds an awful lot like handwriting to me. When they're being kind to you because of handwriting, you know you're in bad shape. If you helped me out and I actually turned in something decent, she'd probably keel over from the shock. Nope, they've got me pegged as a dumb kid by now. It's a little late in the game to start getting smart, I'm afraid."

Laura stopped and grew pensive. She pulled forward a piece of her long hair abstractedly and inspected it. "Could use a washing, couldn't it?" she asked, but from the way she said it, it was clear she wasn't really directing the question to Kate.

"What about the rest of your grades?" Kate asked after a while. "I mean besides the English."

"They're not terrific. English is the worst. If I really pushed it for the rest of the year, I might be able to slide out of here with a high C average. But even that's not really good enough."

"To get into college?"

"Into anyplace decent."

"Which is why you haven't applied."

"Which is why I haven't applied."

"Well, maybe if you don't like studying very much, college isn't really such a terrific idea for you anyway."

"You've sold me. Now all you've got to do is convince the rest of them."

"Like who?"

"Like Bob. He's convinced I'm going to Northern with him. Like Mom and Dad. It's practically all they talk about."

"But they must know about your grades."

"They think I ought to just try to get in on probation somewhere, anywhere, then work to get my grades up and then transfer somewhere better."

"Maybe it's worth a try."

"Kate. I can't even get it together to do one crummy paper on Mark Twain. Do you really think I'd ever make it through four years of college? I mean, I've got a real strong feeling that handwriting doesn't count for too much there."

"But what would you do if you didn't go? Work at the cleaners?"

"For a while maybe. I've got a sort of plan."

Kate didn't say anything.

"Do you want to know what it is?" Laura asked after a while.

"I didn't want to pry."

"It's a much longer shot than college even. What I'd like to do is save up enough to go to New York and take acting lessons. Try to get into the theater. It's about the only thing I'm really sure I'm good at. I know being good in high school plays in Port Williams is a long way from even off-off-off Broadway, but then anybody who's any good now had to start someplace like where I am now. I wouldn't hang around starving for ten years or anything like that, but I could give it a year, don't you think?"

"Why not?"

"Everyone else thinks it's the dumbest idea they've ever heard."

"It's not their life."

Laura smiled to herself. "No it isn't, is

it?" She thought for a while. "It'd be awful tough to do alone, though. The money. Leaving everybody."

"Have you ever done anything hard before?" Kate asked her.

"Sure, lots of stuff. Well, no, not really."

"That's a real solid answer."

"Well, at first I thought, sure I've done tough things. Then I realized that the only one I could come up with was having my appendix out and that was a tough thing I didn't really have any choice about, so I guess it doesn't count. Aside from that I can't think of anything really tough."

"Well, maybe it's time."

"To bite the bullet?"

"To separate the men from the boys. Or rather the women from the girls."

"To put some hair on my chest."

"Right."

"Hey, as long as I'm going to be up all night anyway, maybe you could show me how to highlight my cheekbones."

Chapter 5

Every Thursday when Kate got home from school, there was a letter waiting that her mother had written on Tuesday. Once, the weekly letter didn't come until Friday and Kate had a brief, secret moment of glee, which she didn't quite understand, thinking that her mother hadn't gotten it together to write until Wednesday. Then she looked at the postmark and saw that it was Tuesday as usual, that of course it was the Post Office and not her mother that had gotten off schedule.

Aunt Caroline usually pointed out the letter.

"Letter from your mom on the coffee table," she would say.

"Thanks, Aunt Caroline," Kate would say.

"Aren't you going to read it?" Aunt Caroline would say.

"Oh, I'll get to it later," Kate would say.

Kate figured Aunt Caroline probably thought she was a rotten kid, but what else could she do. She didn't want to say she was taking the letter up to her room to read it. That would just sound too whimpy. And if she read it in the living room, there was always the chance her aunt would come in and find her crying, which is usually what she did when she read her mother's letters.

She wasn't quite sure why they made her cry. Since her mother wasn't at home, they weren't full of stuff like "Oh do we miss you when we gather around the old hearth fire every night," or anything like that, which would have made her homesick. Nor were they full of stuff like "Wish you were here on the sands of Waikiki," which would make her envious at missing all the fun her parents were having without her. Actually, it didn't sound like they were having much fun at all. Most of the letters were on stationery from motels in boring sounding places like Endicott, New York, and Kankakee, Illinois. Without her job and friends and house, her mother seemed a little lost. The letters all had the same forced, cheery tone. Things were always "very interesting" in Endicott or Kankakee or wherever. Daddy was always "working very hard." Her mother was always "taking in the sights" or "picking up the local color." The local color was usually something like "the most marvelous little luncheonette" or "a town square out of Currier and Ives." The sights so far had been a

70

restored pioneer home and a museum with "the largest collection of Indian arrowheads in the Midwest." Kate didn't have to do too much reading between the lines to pick up on the fact that her mother was bored stiff. This wasn't the part of the letters that made her cry, though. It wasn't that she was insensitive. She cried at all sorts of things — books about lost puppies, movies about doomed romances, any story set in an orphanage. And, of course, she would have been upset if her mother were sick, or in trouble. But it was hard to work up a whole lot of emotion over somebody being bored. Especially when they were being bored by a trip they really hadn't had to take, a trip they could have skipped to stay home with their wonderful daughter.

What did make her cry in the letters was the other stuff. Gentle nagging. Little reminders. That Kate should be sure to help with the housework around Aunt Caroline's. That Kate was due for a visit to the dentist, and to make an appointment with the one the Meyers used. Did she have enough pairs of underwear with her, or did Kate want her to buy some and send them? There was at least one thing like this in every letter and it always got to her. Maybe because these things sounded so much more like the way her mother usually talked to her than the travelog parts did. They closed up the distance, made Kate feel her mother was, in a way, nearby, hanging around, watching, interested.

It had taken her a couple of weeks to realize that it was this about the letters that made her cry. What she still hadn't figured out was why. Maybe it wasn't important enough to figure out. She had been crying less lately. And only at predictable times — late at night, on rainy Sunday afternoons. At first she had cried a lot more and had never been able to predict when it would happen. Mostly when she was alone, but a few times the old ducts had started filling up at embarrassing moments. Once in the car on the way to pick up some carry-out chicken with Uncle Frank. Once watching a TV show in the living room with the whole family. It had been a comedy, so she couldn't even use the excuse of crying over something in the story. Aunt Caroline had noticed and Kate had said she had an eyelash stuck in her eye and gone to the bathroom under the pretense of getting it out. After the incident with Uncle Frank in the car she had bought a pair of sunglasses to cover daytime emergencies. Lately, though, she hadn't needed them much. It wasn't so much that she had become happier as that she had stopped being ambushed by little

moments of sadness. Now she more or less
expected them and, even while she was
going through them, knew that they
wouldn't last forever, that they would pass
and things would look better again. She
wondered if she was at sixteen already
getting philosophical. Maybe it was just
that when you're sixteen, so many things
are always going wrong that you have to
be philosophical to survive.

She had been getting along better at the
Meyers' lately. That was one good thing.
Laura had asked her why she was wasting
her time with the karate and découpage
classes.

"Well, I don't want to offend your
mother."

"I don't think you have to worry about
that. Look, she'll drive you nuts if you go
along with every one of her schemes. Maybe
you've noticed that Mom's a little, well, a
little overenthusiastic. She hatches about
a dozen plots a week. She'd just wear you
out if you went along with all of them.
You've got to learn to dodge. Just tell her
you don't have time for the classes anymore."

"Laura, she knows that all I have is
time."

"Just tell her you're tired of them then."

"I don't think I could do that."

"Well then, leave it to me. I know how to handle her."

Laura's method of handling her, which Kate overheard from the kitchen that night, turned out to be telling her mother, "Look, Kate's bored stiff with all these classes. She doesn't want to go anymore."

Miraculously, Aunt Caroline wasn't hurt by this at all.

"Am I glad you told me," Kate heard her tell Laura. "I'm so sick of going every week. The karate leaves me sore for two days afterward. I thought she was loving it, though, and so I didn't want to quit."

And that was the end of the classes for both of them. Since then, whenever Aunt Caroline approached Kate with a terrific idea, of which as Laura had pointed out she had about a dozen a week, Kate felt freer to express her true opinion. And so when it was, "Why don't we just skip dinner tonight and have a banana split party instead," Kate went out and bought the ice cream. And when it was, "Kate, what do you think of unicycles," Kate was fast enough to figure out that it wasn't an academic question, and bold enough to nip it in the bud with, "I think a person would probably break both legs twice before she ever learned to ride it."

After a few weeks of this, Kate and Aunt Caroline had worked into a looser relationship that was easier on both of them.

Uncle Frank had never really been a problem. From the first, he had mostly ignored Kate, which was okay. He seemed to mostly ignore everybody. At the plant, he had some vague, paper-pushing job that didn't seem to interest him very much. At least not enough to talk about it at home. Most nights, he came home from work, read the paper in the living room, had dinner with the rest of them, then went straight down to his basement workshop for the rest of the evening. He spent the better part of the weekend down there too.

Uncle Frank was, in his spare time, an inventor. So far, he had fourteen patents on inventions he hadn't been able to sell to anyone: an electric hammer; a digital egg timer; a car seat for dogs; a musical instrument that, with its various attachments, could be changed from a clarinet to an oboe to a flute; a board game with a one-hundred-page rulebook. Stuff like that. Kate knew about these from Laura. Uncle Frank was secretive about his inventing and wasn't interested in much else, and so most of the time it was as if he wasn't there.

The biggest change had been between Kate and Laura. They talked a lot now. Well, a lot considering how little time

Laura spent at home. The best of these talks took place up in Kate's attic late at night, after Aunt Caroline and Uncle Frank had gone to bed.

A lot of the time they talked about Laura and her dozens of problems, most of which revolved around the college issue, but some of which shot off in all directions. Her weight. Her hair. The possessiveness of her boyfriend Bob. The pukiness of Laura's history teacher, Miss Rayburn. The pukiness of a girl named Alice Ann Crouse, whose sole mission in life, to hear Laura tell it, was to make Laura miserable. Kate probably would have grown bored with all of Laura's problems a lot sooner if she hadn't been so fascinated at finding out that someone as pretty and popular as Laura, someone who a year ago Kate would have thought had it knocked, that someone like this even thought she had problems.

Another reason Kate didn't mind that so much of their conversation revolved around Laura was that Kate could tell she wasn't just being used as a sounding board. Although she couldn't imagine why, Laura always seemed really interested in what Kate had to say, really seemed to respect Kate's opinion. Once she asked Laura why she cared what she thought.

"Because you're smart. You can think through something in a clean, straight line.

I always get snagged somewhere in the middle."

Sometimes they talked about Kate. This was hard for Kate at first, both because she wasn't used to talking about herself, at least not about the stuff that really mattered to her, and because at first she didn't really trust Laura. She was always looking for a sarcastic edge in Laura's tone, or a possible put-down if what she said turned out to be too dumb. When she became more and more sure that Laura wasn't laying any traps for her, she relaxed and began to open up.

What was still bothering Kate the most was the way things were going at school. It wasn't that anyone was being actively crummy to her. She hadn't been picked as easy prey by any Stacy Adamses. It was just that no one seemed to know or care that she was there. This was a hard problem to get across to somebody like Laura, whose main worry was that her social life was eating up all the time she ought to be spending on more important things. How could she explain how much it bothered her that the phone never rang for her to someone who had her mother screen her calls every night and tell half the kids she wasn't home? How could she express her nervousness about dating to someone who was always saying things like, "All these parties are beginning to seem the same to me. I mean, I get there and I think, hey, didn't I just go through this number last weekend. It's always the same kids and the same records and the same big bowls of chips next to the little bowls of sour cream mixed with onion soup mix. A lot of the time lately, I find myself wishing I'd stayed home in front of the tube instead."

And so Kate approached the subject timidly. For the most part, Laura was more sympathetic than she expected. Sympathetic, but not terribly helpful, which was okay. Kate didn't want to be anyone's charity case, dragged along to these "boring" parties, or fixed up with one of Bob's buddies. That would just embarrass her. It would probably even embarrass her if Laura handed down helpful little hints like the teenage magazines did. "Put on a sunny smile." "Be a good listener." "Just be yourself." Dumb advice like this was, Kate figured, the only kind applicable to dumb problems like hers. Still, it did seem like the advice was dumber than the problem.

One night very late, after Kate had turned off the light and was half asleep, she heard Laura bounding up the stairs two at a time.

"Mind if I turn the light on?" she asked Kate as she turned it on. She pulled Kate's desk chair up to the foot of the bed, then sat down, straddling it backwards.

"I've got a terrific idea."

"Oh-oh," Kate said.

"What's the matter?"

"That sounded an awful lot like your mother."

"I swear this has nothing to do with unicycles."

"Oh, in that case."

"You might not go for this right away, but all I want you to do is promise me you'll think about it."

"Okay I promise."

"It's about the drama club."

"I take back my promise."

"Come on. It really is a neat club, as clubs go. Lots of kids belong. It's a real easy way to meet people and they have their own parties on the opening and closing nights of every play. I don't know why I didn't think of it before."

"But I can't act. I get butterflies telling you and your mom and dad a story at dinner."

"You don't have to act. Only maybe half the kids in the club ever get on stage. There's all sorts of other stuff that needs to be done. Make-up and costumes and lighting."

"Laura, I know how these things go.

You're just going merrily along painting a tree on the set and it's the night before the play opens and the female lead gets the flu and overnight they want you to learn the part of Scarlett O'Hara."

"Kate, believe me, there's no chance anybody's going to ask you to do Scarlett O'Hara. Oh, that didn't come out too well, did it? What I meant was that there's so much competition for parts that if you don't want to act, no one's ever going to force you."

"I don't know, Laura. It's already halfway through the year. I mean the club's already formed and everybody knows each other and everything."

"Not true. A whole bunch of new kids came in this semester. But I don't want to pressure you. I just want you to think about it. If you decide you want to give it a try, just let me know and I'll see what they need people for and bring you around."

"It's not that I don't appreciate your trying to help," Kate started to say.

"Just think about it, okay?" Laura cut her short.

"Okay."

A few days later, mostly so that Laura wouldn't think she was a complete social loss, Kate told her she would give it a try.

"Oh, I'm glad," Laura said. "I really

think you'll like it. I'm not all that gung ho a club joiner or anything, and I really like it. We do some pretty good stuff, you know. Right now, we're rehearsing *The Little Foxes*. Do you know it?"

"Sounds like animal fables."

"You're thinking of *The Three Little Pigs*." Laura laughed. "No, *Little Foxes* is a Lillian Hellman play. It's about a vicious, conniving Southern family."

"What's your part?"

"I'm the loony wife of one of the brothers. I auditioned for the lead, but guess who got it, of course."

"Alice Ann Crouse."

"That twit. She did everything but lick Mr. Herbert's boots to get the part. Someone told me she knitted stocking caps for both his kids and brought them over to his house on Christmas."

"Do you believe that?"

"I wouldn't put it past her. I don't think it was even that she wanted the part so much as it was that she knew how much I wanted it."

"Well, real talent always wins out in the end."

"How do you know I've got real talent? You've never seen me in anything."

"I don't know. Maybe you do. Maybe you don't. Maybe you do, but not quite enough. I think trying to make it in New

York is going to be real tough. But you've got all the Alice Ann Crouses beat already just because you care about this so much more than they do. I guess you'll have to worry about all the others like you when you get to New York."

"*If* I get there."

"I don't see how a one-way plane ticket would be that big a problem."

"No. But it'd mean giving up everything I've got going here."

"I don't suppose that means the job at the cleaners, so we must be talking about Bob."

"Do you still want to work there?" Laura asked. She did this a lot — changed the subject suddenly — not so much on purpose, but because her mind had slipped into another gear.

"Sure. I thought you were going to ask about me."

"Yeah, well, they didn't really need anybody until now. Roseanne is going to quit. Her grades are slipping. So if you still want it, I can ask Gomez tomorrow. I think he'd just need you on Saturdays."

"It's not too hard?"

"No. Just boring."

"For money, I can be bored."

"Okay, I'll ask him then."

"So what about Bob?"

"He thinks we ought to get married and

go to college together. You know — live in one of those shabby, furnished apartments and get part-time jobs and live on casseroles and study all night.One of those ideas that'd be romantic for about two weeks."

"I didn't know it was that heavy a deal between you two."

"It is with him. For me it's, well, it's more complicated. It's something I'm scared to lose right now, but on the other hand, it doesn't seem like enough for a lifetime commitment. I mean I like him enough for after basketball practice on Tuesday nights, and for going out on weekends, but I'm not sure I'd like him every day for the rest of my life. He's cute and all — fun and easy to be with and I like making out with him when we park out on the bluff, but I don't know. It's complicated. Like, I think I've already heard all his jokes. We're on the second time around on most of them and we've only been going together six months. And he wants six kids. One seems like a lot to me. And he loves Port Williams, loves the idea of living in a small town. I've wanted to get to the city since I was about three."

"It doesn't sound like too great a meeting of minds," Kate said.

"That's another thing. Aside from telling dumb jokes, he's pretty smart. Real smart, I think. Especially in science and stuff. At any rate, he's a lot smarter than me. He doesn't see that now. We just do the same things everyone else does and hang out with the same crowd. The brain level there is not terrifically high and so I don't stand out as a dummy or anything. But if we went to college together, he'd begin to see. Then we'd get out of school and move back here, or to some other dinky burg. He wants to be a research chemist. He'd be off all day with interesting people and I'd be home with the six kids. I think I want more than that. Or at least different from that."

"Yeah." Kate couldn't think of what else to say.

"Hey!" It was Laura's standard subject-changer. "If you really want to come tomorrow, meet me backstage in the auditorium after last period. I'll be looking for you."

Chapter 6

The next afternoon, Kate went down to the auditorium to meet Laura as planned. She came in from the back and she could see Laura onstage with two boys and Mr. Herbert, the boys' gym teacher who also served as drama coach. They were all holding scripts and, as the characters read through their parts, Mr. Herbert would interrupt to show them a gesture they should be using, or push them over to wherever they should be.

Kate sat down at the end of a row about halfway back from the stage. She didn't suppose there was any sense in going backstage if Laura wasn't there. And it was sort of fun, sitting in the shadows where no one could see her, being an unseen audience of one.

The part of the scene they were working on was very short, but it took a long time — maybe fifteen runthroughs — before Mr. Herbert seemed to be satisfied that everyone at least knew which lines were his, and wasn't likely to walk off the edge of the stage.

Kate stayed in her seat for a few minutes, fighting off the urge to just take off and go home now that the easy part was over. But in the end, not wanting Laura to think she was more out of it than she probably already did, she got her books off the seat next to her and reluctantly found her way to the backstage area.

Sitting out front, Kate had assumed that Mr. Herbert, Laura, and the two boys were the only people around. And so she was stunned when she opened the door to the din of maybe thirty-five kids rushing around in various activities — painting backdrops, designing sets, sewing costumes, reading their parts to each other — all of them looking like they knew very much what they were doing. Laura was in the wings, talking with one of the boys who had been in the scene with her. Kate waited for them to be done, then when it looked like they never were going to finish, got up her courage and went over.

"Hey, Kate," Laura said. "I didn't think you were going to show up."

"I said I would," Kate said.

"Yeah, well, you know, I thought ... hey, Kate, this is Jim Spahn."

"Hi. I was watching you both go through that last scene."

"Pretty grim, wasn't it?" Laura said. "Of course, acting with Jim makes it tough on the rest of us. We just keep him in the club in case we need a fox terrier impersonation."

Both Laura and Jim cracked up at this. Kate tried to laugh along, without having any idea what the joke was.

"Kate's thinking about joining the club," Laura told Jim. "I've got to check with Herbert about getting her on an assignment."

Before she could do anything, though, a skinny, sour-faced girl came up to them with, Kate thought, an "I'm at my wit's end" look on her face. Kate felt like a prophet when the girl said: "Laura, I'm at my wit's end. Miss Horwich sent me to get you for a costume fitting half an hour ago."

"What am I supposed to do?" Laura asked her, "break in the middle of the scene because the Witch issues one of her summonses? I'll go now. Kate, just hang around for a few minutes, will you? The Witch'll blow a fuse if I don't get back there."

Without waiting for an answer she was off, with the sour-faced girl following her like a detective. Kate turned to fill in the time making some small talk with the guy named Jim, but found he had slipped off somewhere.

And so for the next twenty minutes she stood where she was. Although nobody looked at her as if she were anything but an inanimate obstacle, she had never felt more conspicuous or self-conscious. Surely they must all be wondering what she was doing here. Even she was wondering what she was doing here. What if Laura didn't get done with her fitting for an hour? What if she had forgotten about Kate completely and never came back? Kate had just about made up her mind to go home and tell Laura later that she had gotten a sudden stomach ache when the door burst open behind her, letting in a gust of snow and a big blond guy with very red cheeks and a plaid lumber jacket to match.

The force of the door threw Kate forward and made her spill her armful of books on the floor.

"Hey, I'm sorry," he said. "I didn't mean to knock you out or anything. Here, let me pick those up for you." Handing the books back to her, he said, "You haven't seen Bill around anywhere, have you?"

"Uh, I'm just waiting for my cousin. I don't really know anybody here."

"Well, I guess I'd better go look for him. Sorry again."

"That's okay."

She watched him walk away with enormous strides and swinging arms. She thought that he probably bumped into all sorts of things and people every day. Almost as soon as he was gone he was back again, this time with Mr. Herbert who was handing him a clipboard full of papers.

"Just see how much of this list you can talk them out of," Mr. Herbert was saying.

"Okay. I sure wish I could find Bill. He said he'd be able to come along and help me." Then noticing Kate again, he asked, "He didn't come by here while I was gone, did he?"

"I don't think so. Like I told you, I wouldn't know him if I did see him."

"Oh, that's right, you're just waiting for your sister."

"Cousin."

At this, Mr. Herbert looked at Kate as if she had just materialized.

"Are you Laura Meyers' cousin?"

"Yes."

"She told me you were here. I'm supposed to find something for you to do."

"Hey, Mr. Herbert. I'm going to take off now. I've only got my dad's truck for two hours and I can't waste any more time waiting around for the idiot."

"Tell you what, Andy. Why don't you take . . ." He looked at Kate questioningly. She couldn't tell what he wanted. "What's your name?" he finally asked her.

"Kate."

"Why don't you take Kate here along for the ride? She's new to the club."

"Sure. Okay."

"Great. See you kids later then." And he was off.

"Where are we going?" Kate asked Andy.

"Some furniture store is going to lend us some props if we put their name in the program. I've got to go over and pick the stuff up."

"I really don't think I'd be a terrific help loading furniture."

"Oh, I can handle the heavy stuff. You can help decide what looks old and Southern."

"I guess I could do that."

"Well, come on then. If I don't have this truck back in two hours, my dad'll have my skin."

At first, Kate couldn't think of anything to say. Apparently, he couldn't either, or maybe he didn't want to be bothered talking to her. The silence made her uncomfortable and she guessed it made him a little nervous too, because after a while he turned the radio on. That eased things a little. At least it made Kate feel less like he was someone she was sitting next to in the doctor's waiting room.

"My name's Andy," he said.

"Yeah, I heard Mr. Herbert."

"And you're Kate."

"Yeah."

Brilliant conversation, Kate thought.

"I haven't seen you around," he said. She figured she'd better come up with something better than "yeah" or he'd probably give up on her entirely.

"I just moved here. I'm staying with my cousin until the summer. She thinks the drama club is real neat and sort of talked me into coming down today."

"It's okay, I guess. Better than most of the clubs, I guess. I can't really see joining any of them, though."

"Then why are you out here driving through a foot of snow and loading furniture and all that?"

"Oh, I don't really belong to the club. I just help out when they need me. I think I'm the only one they could find with a truck. And a generous nature. My friend Bill is in the club. Thinks he's going to be the next Robert Redford."

"Will he?"

Andy looked over at Kate. "Well, if his face clears up and his hair starts going blond and he grows six inches, then I think he might have a chance. Then he'd only have to worry about the fact that he can't act."

Kate laughed. "And this poor guy thinks you're his friend?"

"I am. I'm a terrific friend. I figure I'm doing him a favor by letting him know how terrible he is before he wastes all his money running off to Hollywood or something. Well, here we are."

In the furniture store, Kate began to feel useful. She wondered what the sets would have looked like if she hadn't been along. First he thought the Danish modern looked "real tough." When she pointed out that it wasn't old enough looking, he asked her what she thought of the Mediterranean display.

At that point, a salesman came over to them.

"Looking for some starter pieces?" he asked.

"Huh?" Andy said.

"Well, I gather you two are newlyweds."

The red on Andy's cheeks spread over his entire face. Kate hoped she wasn't blushing as hard as he was. He started stammering.

"Hey, no. We're just from the high school. We're supposed to see Mr. Bertani." He shoved the clipboard list at the salesman, as if it were self-explanatory.

"You kids are buying furniture for the school?" the salesman asked.

"No, props for the play are all we want.

Mr. Bertani is supposed to know all about it."

"Well, kids, I haven't been filled in on this. Let me go check it out with Mr. Bertani. Just have a look around and I'll be right back."

Kate led Andy around the store, but couldn't find anything that looked quite right. She supposed they probably didn't make furniture like the stuff she had seen in *Gone with the Wind* and other movies about the old South. Early American seemed too Northern. The closest she could come was a display of French Provincial.

"I think this'll have to do," she told Andy. "It's not the right thing, but I think it's the closest."

The salesman found Mr. Bertani, who came out from the back and was only going to lend them a sofa, an easy chair, and a coffee table until Andy promised him a full-page ad in the program and pointed out that in three nights 1,200 parents and relatives — all potential furniture buyers — would see the program and spend three hours looking at a set full of Bertani furniture. This little sales pitch — which Kate found rather amazing — netted them an extra loveseat, end tables, three lamps, two chairs, and a rug. Andy helped the guys at the store load it all in the truck and all the kids in the club pitched in unloading it onto the stage. By the time it was all done, it was nearly 6:30 and Andy had to get the truck back to his dad.

"If you want to ride back to my house, I can pick up my car and give you a lift from there," he told her.

Kate thought he was just being nice.

"Oh, that's okay. Laura's still around and so I can walk home with her."

"Bet she won't stop off and buy you a Coke on the way."

Kate couldn't believe he was sort of asking her out. Except for saying fascinating things like, "Do you think the tarp is tied tight enough so none of the furniture is getting snowed on?" she had hardly spoken to him since they started back from the store. He couldn't possibly think she was interesting. And with her old coat on and her hair all frizzed up from having been snowed on, he couldn't possibly think she was cute.

"Okay," was all she could say, then realized that probably sounded like she was bored with the whole idea. Which she wasn't. "I'd better tell Laura, though, so my aunt doesn't hold dinner for me."

They went to the McDonald's. She had a small Coke. He had two Big Macs, a large order of fries, a milk shake, and apple pie.

"Won't that spoil your dinner?" she

asked him, then felt stupid for asking. If he had wanted nagging, he would have invited his parents along.

"My mom works 3:00 to 7:00 at the hospital. Most nights, she's too bushed to cook. I figure a Big Mac's probably no worse than a TV dinner. It's all the same chemicals and additives molded into different shapes is all. If the coach saw me eating all this junk, he'd probably throw me off the team. I'm supposed to be having steak and salad every night until the meet Friday."

"You're on the track team?"

"Swimming."

"Isn't belonging to the swim team sort of like joining a club?" As soon as she said it, she was sorry. Even when she was just trying to make pleasant small talk, it always seemed to come out wrong. He probably thought she was baiting him.

"Well, it's just sort of practical. To swim competitively, you have to join the team. Once you're on it, though — once you're in a race — it's an individual sport. It's just you against the other guys, even the ones on your own team. You care about your team winning, but you want to place first and have the other guy finish second."

"So it's easier to be a star in something like swimming?"

"Not really. The guys who play football

and basketball around here get a lot more attention, if that's what you mean by 'star.' The thing with swimming is more private. It's knowing real clearly how well you've done, because you've done it all by yourself. With basketball and football, you can do everything right and still lose the point because someone else along the way fouls up. But even if we lose a meet, I can still cop a few ribbons, hang them over my bed, and know that I did all right anyway."

"Sounds almost un-American," she said.

He laughed and Kate was glad he had picked up that she was just teasing.

"I know," he said. "I think the school's probably got me under investigation for a subversive attitude toward sports. Hey, you know, you really ought to come and see the meet Friday. Do you like swimming?"

"I don't know. I really don't know much about it."

"What's to know? It's just four guys trying to get across a pool as fast as possible."

"That much I guess I could get a grip on. But different strokes and stuff. I don't know anything about all that. I never learned to swim myself."

"That's impossible. Everyone knows how to swim."

"Not me."

"But how did you manage to get out of it?"

"Oh, my parents sent me down to the park one summer when I was a kid to get some lessons. They just didn't take on me, though. I did a pretty good dead man's float, but when they got up to dog paddling and blowing bubbles, I knew I wouldn't make it and dropped out."

"And you haven't gone swimming at all since then?"

"Not a stroke."

"How could you avoid it?"

"Oh, it hasn't been too hard to get around it. When I go to the lake, I just stay on the beach. I only fill the bathtub halfway. I never go on vacation to Mississippi during the flood season."

"Yeah, but how are you going to feel when you're out sailing someday and come across a boatload of drowning orphans, and won't be able to do anything about saving them?"

"I guess I'll be glad they're orphans so I won't have to tell their parents I had to let them all drown."

This cracked him up. Kate couldn't believe how easy it was. She didn't think it had been a particularly funny joke. Whatever she had thought about talking to boys, she hadn't thought it was going to be easy like this. Just as she was thinking this, it did turn difficult. When he stopped laughing, he didn't seem about to say anything. She tried to think of something to start the conversation going again, but her mind went numb. He was still eating, but Kate had finished her Coke and had to just sit there, pushing the ice in the bottom of the paper cup around with her straw.

"I've never seen you around in classes or anything," she finally said. "I guess you're a senior."

"Yeah."

"How do you like it? I mean your classes and teachers and all?"

"Well, I guess it's like you and swimming. School doesn't seem to take on me very well."

"You're not flunking out or anything?"

"Naw, my grades are okay. It's just that I have to spend too much time to get them. Too much time studying a whole bunch of stuff that doesn't interest me."

"Are you going to college next year?"

"Yeah, probably. If I want to coach swimming, I've got to get a Phys. Ed. degree. I'm accepted at State. I don't know. I figure I'll decide over the summer. My dad's got a garage, and I might just stick around next year and work for him. I like working on cars. He's not crazy about me not going away to school, but he'll give me the job if I want it. You sure ask a lot of questions."

"Sorry."

"No, that's okay. It's just a little unusual. Some of the girls around here, all they do is talk about themselves. 'Hey, does my hair look all right?' 'I could've died when I got called on in history this afternoon. I was writing a note to Marsha and didn't even hear the question.' You know. They rattle on like someone's got a gun at their back saying 'Keep talking.' You're different."

"It's just that I don't have all that much to say."

"Yeah, sure."

"It's true. I hardly ever have anything to say to anybody."

"That's funny. You look to me like a person who has a whole lot going on in her head."

"Oh yeah, my head is full of stuff. It's just that whenever I think of saying it out loud, I stop and wonder if it's too dumb, or if I'll say it wrong, or if they'll understand, or if it's worth mentioning at all. By the time I go through all that, even if I've decided to say something, the other person is usually on to something else."

"I guess I'm the opposite. I say anything I feel like saying, then wait for my brain to catch up to see if I'm sorry I said it."

"I think I'd rather be like you," Kate said.

"I was just thinking I'd rather be like you," he said.

They both laughed.

"Hey, we'd better get going," he said, looking at his watch. "I've got practice at 8:00."

He drove her home. When they pulled up in the driveway, she got her books together and opened the door on her side.

"Thanks for the Coke," she said, and got out.

"See you," he called from inside the car. "You going to come to the meet Friday night?"

"I don't know. I'll try."

Walking up the ice-slicked driveway to the side door, she slipped and fell, dropping her books all over for the second time that day. She looked up and was glad to see he had already rounded the corner and was out of sight.

Chapter 7

Kate would have gone to the meet Friday night if she could have talked Laura into going with her.

"Gee, Kate," was Laura's response when Kate asked her, "I'd love to, but I sort of told Karen I'd come over and listen to some of her new records."

Kate didn't push it. She knew that if she did, she could probably talk her into it. Laura went over to Karen's about three times a week and so it wasn't a big commitment. And she sat through basketball games all the time for Bob, so she could probably endure one swim meet for Kate. Still, to get her to go, Kate would have to make a big deal out of it, and she didn't particularly want to do that. Laura had been rabidly curious about Kate and Andy ever since the night they had gone to McDonald's. It turned out Laura had gone out with him once last year, liked him pretty well, and been bothered by the fact that he had never called again. She told Kate he was probably stuck-up. Kate didn't think he was stuck-up at all, but she didn't say anything.

Apparently Andy was something of a mystery around school. Laura told Kate he was popular, but didn't seem to care about that sort of thing. All the guys liked him, but he didn't hang around with any particular crowd. He took out a lot of girls, but dropped them after one or two dates. Laura couldn't remember him ever going with anyone for any length of time. He might show up at a party and be the center of attention for the whole night, or he might come late and hang around the edges and leave after an hour of not saying much to anybody. Or he might say he'd come and then not show up at all.

And so when Kate came back from McDonald's that night, Laura quizzed her like crazy. What did they talk about? Was he nice? What was he wearing? Did Kate like him? Did she think he liked her? Did he try to kiss her? Kate felt like a spy being interrogated. Still, she probably would have been more flattered than embarrassed by Laura's interest if she didn't know from how much Laura gossiped about her friends that she was probably stockpiling this information just so she could pass it on to Karen and Cindy and Joy. It gave Kate the creeps to think of being the subject of discussion at the next dirt-digging session in the girls' locker room. And so since then she had tried to downplay the whole thing.

The other reason she didn't want to make a big deal about going to the meet and dragging Laura along was that she didn't want to be embarrassed in front of her once they got there. Andy had only said he hoped she would come. He hadn't said he would see her there, or anything. Since Kate had never before expressed any interest in swimming, Laura of course knew that Kate didn't want to go just for the sport of it. What if they went and Andy never even saw her? Or saw her and just disappeared afterward with the other guys. Or worse, with another girl. Kate would look like a fool for having come, and she didn't want Laura to see that. On the other hand, she couldn't possibly go alone. Someone else could probably do it without a thought. For Kate, it was impossible.

So, when Friday night came and Laura asked her at dinner what time she was leaving for the meet, she told her she had decided to bag it.

"I've got a book report due Monday and haven't even started the book." In case that hadn't sounded like enough of an excuse, she added, "Besides, I decided to waterproof my boots and they're in the middle of the drying stage."

She realized, as she was saying it, that this last part was probably the dumbest excuse anyone had ever made for not going somewhere. And so she wasn't surprised when Laura flashed her a "you pathetic chicken" look. At least Laura had the good grace not to say anything. All Aunt Caroline needed to hear was that Kate was shying away from the first faint glimmer of a social life that had come her way in Port Williams. She would be in her coat in five minutes, ready to escort Kate personally. And if there was one thing more excruciatingly embarrassing to Kate than the idea of showing up at the meet alone, it was the idea of showing up with Aunt Caroline. Luckily, Aunt Caroline accepted the inane excuses.

The next day was Saturday — Kate's first day at Schmidt Cleaners. Nobody remembered Schmidt, if there ever was a Schmidt. For years now, the place had been owned by Gomez.

Gomez gave Kate the creeps. He was old and short and stooped and had brown teeth from the tobacco he chewed constantly, spitting it into the large tin cans he had placed all around the shop. He let Laura show Kate the ropes, but came around two or three times during the morning to give Kate a sideways fish-eye, like he half expected to catch her with her hand in the till.

"I don't think he likes me," Kate told Laura when Gomez was out of earshot.

"Oh, I'm sure he thinks you're fine."

"I don't think I like him."

"That's more reasonable. Who *could* like Gomez, after all? Except maybe his banker. I'll bet he's got millions by now, the way he pinches pennies."

Schmidt's did seem to be a low overhead operation, with none of the fancy modernization or even up-front decorating Kate was used to seeing in cleaners. The patched linoleum floor and homemade-looking wooden counter and ancient cash register all seemed to date from at least fifty years ago. The wooden counter was all that separated the front of the shop from the cluttered recesses of the back, with all its racks of cleaned clothes and bins of dirty ones and the fumy dry-cleaning machines and the steamy pressing table manned by the old Chinese man Yin.

At least the work was easy. Kate learned everything she was supposed to know in a couple of hours. By noon, she was already bored.

"How can you stand this?" she asked Laura.

"Just wait 'til you get that nice little wad of cash this afternoon."

In addition to being bored, Kate was

105

getting a little queasy around the edges, probably from the cleaning fumes and steam wafting up from the back of the shop.

Laura was waiting on a customer — a woman who had spilled permanent black ink on a pair of white slacks and was indignant that they hadn't been able to get it all out. When she finally left — muttering threats about taking her business elsewhere — Kate told Laura she was getting a little woozy.

"It's probably because you haven't eaten anything yet. Why don't you take half an hour and go across the street to the snack shop. Just don't order their chicken salad. They use that stuff from a roll that tastes like pressed toad."

When Kate got there, she took a stool at the end of the counter near the front door. The snack shop was one of those places where you just know the food is going to taste as cardboardy as the furniture looks.

Kate ordered a bacon, lettuce, and tomato sandwich and a Coke, figuring there wasn't too much they could do to ruin either. To pass the time until her order came up, she pulled a paperback out of her purse. It was a new Gothic romance she had just started and was still in the part where the heroine, Claudia, is living a nice, safe, dull life with her parents on their farm in France. Kate had read enough of these books to know that nothing was going to be nice or safe or dull for Claudia for more than fifteen more pages. And so she was skimming rapidly, not noticing who had come in along with the blast of cold air that hit her when the restaurant door opened behind her. It wasn't until her sandwich came that she looked down the counter and saw Andy sitting there having a cup of coffee.

It was an awkward situation. Maybe he hadn't seen her. She could hardly expect him to recognize her all scrunched down in her winter coat. She should probably say hi or something. On the other hand, he had been sitting there a while. If he hadn't said anything by now, it might be that he was ignoring her. She didn't know what to do and so followed her usual course of doing nothing. She finished her sandwich in a hurry, counted out the exact amount plus a tip and put it on the top of the check in front of her, picked up her hat and mittens and got up to leave. He must have caught her moving out of the corner of his eye. He turned to look just as she turned to get off the stool. Face to face, not more than ten feet apart, there wasn't much chance of sneaking out.

"Hi," was all she could think of to say.

"Hi," he said flatly, then immediately turned back to his cup of coffee.

She felt like a sharp, thin knife was going through her. She walked out of the restaurant and back to the cleaners. The afternoon was a blur. Twice she made the wrong change for customers and once she gave out the wrong package of shirts. When they were getting ready to close up and leave at 6:00, she heard Laura telling Gomez that her cousin was just a little slow catching on, that she was sure she would have a better grip next Saturday. Kate guessed Laura was working hard to keep her from getting fired.

"What got into you this afternoon?" Laura asked when they were on their way home.

"Nothing."

"Oh, come on. I want to know what's going on in that fevered brain of yours."

"It was at the restaurant."

"You had the chicken salad. I knew it."

"No. Not the restaurant. *At* the restaurant. I ran into Andy."

"And?"

"Two hi's — mine and his."

"That was it?"

"It won't make Guinness as the world's longest conversation."

"You should've gone to the meet last night."

"Probably."

"For sure."

"Hey, quit looking at me like I just pressed the atomic bomb button. I don't know why this bothers you. It doesn't bother me all that much. It just isn't that big a deal."

"You're right. Hell, you got your boots waterproofed last night. That's much more important."

"Come on, Laura. Lay off me, will you? I already feel like a jerk about this."

"You could probably patch it up."

"No. *You* could probably patch it up if it was you. But we're talking here about the original, patented, government-inspected, certified Grade-A social turkey."

"Maybe I could help out. Sort of explain to him how it happened. Real casual like. Nothing obvious or embarrassing."

"Like the real casual way you told your mom I was bored stiff with her classes? Thanks anyway."

"No, this one I think I could work real smooth. I'm already getting a terrific idea."

"Kill it before it grows. Please. I'd rather handle this myself."

"Which means you won't handle it at all."

"Give me a chance."

"Okay. I'll hold off for a while and see what happens. Then, if by some chance you forget or don't have time to get around to it, I'll take care of it for you."

"Terrific."

Kate just couldn't really bring herself to do anything about the situation. Calling him was out of the question. That would be embarrassing and nervous-making. And no more casual way out came to mind. She didn't know where he hung out, or who he hung out with, so she couldn't really work up a plan of just being somewhere she could be sure he would turn up. And even if he did turn up, she couldn't really imagine what she could say to him. After half an hour of heavyweight thinking on the subject, she gave up. As far as she could see, it was a hopeless situation. Maybe Laura would forget, or Andy's family would move out of town, or a tornado would level Port Williams. Those seemed to be her only chances of getting out of this.

Chapter 8

On the next Saturday, Kate and Laura took off from the cleaners a couple of hours early so they could make the Drama Club bus trip to Crane College to see its Shakespeare Festival production of *Hamlet*. Laura had been hopped up about it all week.

"Now you'll get a chance to see how the big kids play," was what she told Kate on Monday. On Tuesday, she told her about all the time and expense they threw into productions at Crane. Wednesday, it was a monolog that took up the whole five blocks to school — all about how tough it was to get into the drama program at Crane, and how many big names in the theater had come out of there. On Thursday, she seemed to have run out of steam on the subject, but then on Friday night, just before she left on a date with Bob, Laura came up to Kate's room, bounding up the stairs by twos, rushing in out of breath, like the person in Japanese horror movies who comes in to tell everybody that the monster is gobbling up Tokyo.

"I can't believe I forgot to tell you this part. Do you know who's directing this thing?"

"Who?"

"Guess."

"I couldn't. Really."

"Harold Braithwaite. He's teaching for just this one semester at Crane. I mean Harold Braithwaite. Can you believe it?"

"It's hard."

Kate didn't have the vaguest idea who Harold Braithwaite was, but she sure hoped he was good. And that all the actors showed up. And that the costumes didn't get lost at the cleaners. And that none of the scenery fell down in the middle of Act II. Not that Kate cared for her own sake. She liked plays fine, but she couldn't imagine that anything that had ever happened on any stage was as good as Laura was expecting this to be. And so for her, this play had better be perfect.

At the last minute, Laura talked Bob into coming along.

"He'll only go if we take his car. He says he rides the bus to every away game, and isn't about to spend a free Saturday night riding sixty miles each way steeped in the smell of sweat socks."

"So I'll see you up there."

112

"Don't be silly. You can ride up with us."

"But he won't want me tagging along."

"You don't get car sick, do you? Or want to play 'Count the Gas Stations' all the time?"

"Laura."

"Then he'll be crazy about having you along."

"But . . ."

"Stop worrying."

"Okay. Okay."

And so Kate went with them, and was surprised to find that Bob really didn't seem to mind. But then, he was so obviously crazy about Laura, he probably would have been amenable to her bringing a rhinoceros along in the back seat.

She could see why Laura was having a hard time tearing herself away from him. In addition to being so good looking Kate had to try to keep from staring at him all the time, he was one of the few guys she had ever met who was easy to talk to right off the bat. But then probably part of it was knowing that he was already Laura's boyfriend. If she were out on a date with him tonight, she would probably be plunged into her usual chasm of desperate silence.

"Laura didn't by any chance mention to you how terrific this thing tonight was going to be, did she?" Bob asked her.

Laura was driving because she loved Bob's Fiat. Kate was squooshed into a space in the back that might have comfortably held a midget or two cocker spaniels, but was not nearly big enough for a whole, full-sized person. As four-on-the-floor shifting seemed to take up all of Laura's attention, Bob draped himself over the back of his seat and spent most of the trip talking to Kate.

They made it up to Crane almost an hour before curtain time, and the bus from school was nowhere yet in sight. Laura wanted to try to get backstage to talk with Harold Braithwaite, and so Bob suggested that he and Kate take a walk around the campus to fill in the time.

"Pretty," he said after they had been walking a while.

"Huh?"

"Up here. Too bad they don't have an engineering program. Northern's got a terrific one, but it's the pits as campuses go. And full of guys. Because of the engineering school and the agriculture school and the business school. I'm trying to talk Laura into coming up with me."

"She told me."

"She doesn't want to go."

"I know she'd like to be with you."

"But that's not enough."

114

"She never said that. I guess I was just thinking it wouldn't be enough for me. I mean if I had a boyfriend, I don't think being with him would be my only goal in life. But then it's all in the abstract for me. If I were in love with somebody, maybe nothing else would seem important."

"I guess that's sort of what I want from Laura. Maybe it's unrealistic, though. Like I really think I love her, but I've got to get my own life in gear too. I mean there's no way I'd go to New York and hang around waiting for her to become a star. Sometimes it just seems like it should be different for girls, though. I mean she doesn't have to have a career."

"I don't think we're talking about have-to's. This is just something she really wants. And since she's bucking you and her folks and all the odds to go after it, I think, well, I think she probably ought to be taken seriously about it."

"I guess."

"And I don't know much about these things, but I'd guess that miserable girls don't make terrific wives."

"So I should be a big-hearted guy and let her go."

"Do you have any choice?"

They came to a square surrounded by classroom buildings. There was a fountain in the center with benches around it.

"Looks like this is the place where people on the campus tour stop and say 'why don't we sit down here for a minute,' " he said.

"I know. Why don't we sit down here for a minute?" Kate said.

"Good idea."

They didn't say anything for a while, but for once, it didn't feel awkward. It was more like a time for not saying anything rather than a gap between things Kate felt she ought to be saying.

"So what about you?" Bob asked after a while.

"What *about* me?"

"Well, what's your story? I bet you don't have any problems with life plans."

"That's because I'm only a junior. When you're a junior, no one expects you to have a life plan yet."

"How long are you going to be here? I don't mean on this bench. How long are you staying with Laura?"

"Until my folks come and rescue me. Sometime in the summer."

"You don't like it here?"

"It's okay."

"I guess it was tough having your whole life — all your friends and everything — whipped out from under you like that."

"Well, I didn't really have anything that terrific going back home, so it's okay here. I'm just sort of waiting it out."

116

"You're talking about almost a whole year of your life."

"So?"

"Well, it just seems like sort of a waste to wait it out."

"You've got a better idea?"

"Well, I don't know what you're into."

"Not much."

"Then maybe you could. Get into something, that is."

"Like?"

"Well — I know you're probably going to say you're too short, but I've never thought that was all that important."

"Too short for what?"

"Girls' volleyball. It's our weakest team."

Kate began to see what Laura meant about Bob's limitations.

The cold and what looked like the beginning of a snowstorm decided them on getting back to the auditorium.

"There's the bus from school," he said. "We'd better hurry so we can get some seats with everybody else."

When they got inside, they found the rest of the kids fast enough, but Laura wasn't anywhere to be seen. Who was to be seen — at the opposite end of the row where Bob put Kate to save three seats while he went off to wrest Laura from backstage rapture — was Andy.

Luckily, he was with a bunch of guys, punching and poking each other and climbing over seats in what looked to be some long-running rearrangement joke, the lot of them looking like the least likely group of Shakespeare fans ever assembled. Kate slid down in her seat, pretended to be preoccupied looking over her program, and hoped she could get away with not being noticed.

Soon enough, Bob came back with Laura in tow so she had someone to talk to, and soon enough after that, the lights dimmed and the curtain went up and she figured she was home free.

Until intermission.

She stayed in her seat for most of it, talking to Laura, or rather listening to Laura rhapsodize on the first act. Finally, she decided that she had really better make a trip up to the john. When she got there, there was still a long line. By the time she got out, the second act had begun and the lobby had emptied out. Except for him. Leaning against the wall, aimlessly tossing a crushed orange drink carton up in the air and catching it one-handed.

There was nothing to do but go over and say hi. Which she did. And he did.

"I think it's started," she said. "The play."

"So?"

"Don't you want to see how it ends?"

"He dies."

"Hamlet?"

"Yeah. Bill told me."

"I think there's more to it than that. I think with Shakespeare, the fun is in the getting there."

"It's not fun for me. Everyone talks funny."

"Shakespeare probably would've thought you talk funny."

"That's his problem."

"So. You're just going to stand out here practicing your juggling for the next hour?"

"Nope. I'm going to take you for a ride and find out why you don't like me."

"No."

"No, you won't go for a ride?"

"No. I meant no, I don't not like you."

"Is that a roundabout way of saying you like me?"

"Sort of. I guess it is."

"You sure have a funny way of showing it."

"The thing the other night was, well, it was just complicated. It didn't really have anything to do with you."

"You want to tell me about it?"

"You still want to go for that ride?"

"Sure. Let's go. I know you're going to be disappointed, but I don't have my dad's truck tonight. I had to bring my car."

He let her in, then went around and got in on the driver's side. He started it up, then sat for a minute letting it warm up, playing with the heater controls.

He turned to look at her. "You ever been up here before?"

"Un uh."

"Me either. Let's do some exploring."

It had snowed a couple of inches while they were inside. Out on the highway, the clear sky and the white-covered fields reflecting back off the headlights made the night startlingly bright.

"So," he said when they had been driving awhile, "you were going to tell me about your allergy to chlorine."

"Huh?"

"The reason you couldn't come to the meet."

"Oh."

"It really *is* complicated?"

"No, it's just dumb. I didn't have anyone to go with and I'm sort of chicken about doing new things alone."

"But you knew I was going to be there."

"Yes. But you were going to be in the pool."

"I guess I sort of see. Like if I'd told you

where I'd meet you after or something like that, you would have had a little more to grab onto."

"Yeah."

"Sounds reasonable."

"It doesn't. It sounds dumb."

"I'll grant you some people might have been a little more adventurous about the whole thing. But then you're not some people. You're you."

"You make it sound like it's okay."

"I don't know. I guess it's probably a little uncomfortable for you — being shy and all — but I don't think it's a big deal or anything. Like it's one of those things — you know it probably won't last forever, but then again, it probably won't be gone when you get up tomorrow morning. I guess it's just one of those things you've got to hang in with for a while."

"I guess. Are you usually so smart about things?"

"Just the opposite. I'm usually so dumb about things, I don't notice them enough to get bothered about them. Everyone else is worried as hell about stuff and it's like I'm always just waking up saying, 'Duh, what's happening?' "

"Not true."

"It is. Really. What do you say we get off the highway up here and see what's up some of these back roads?"

"We don't have much time, do we? If I don't get back by the time the play's over, Laura's going to think I got swallowed up by a black hole."

"What's a black hole?"

"Something in outer space. You drive your inter-galactic cruiser into one and you're gone for good."

"Well, if there aren't any of them lurking around here, I ought to be able to get you back in time."

They turned off the highway and took so many lefts and rights and forks, Kate couldn't see how they could possibly find their way back before Tuesday. When they finally dead-ended on a gravel road between two farm fields, and facing a third, he shifted into Park and turned the ignition off.

"I thought you might want to stop for a while and enjoy the view," he said, turning toward her, putting his arm up on the back of the seat.

"But there isn't any view here."

He looked around in mock surprise. "Gee, so there isn't."

"Then what are we doing here?"

"You haven't been around much, have you?"

"Not too."

"We are, to use the common colloquialism, parking."

"Oh."

"You've never done it."

"No."

"Take my word for it, you'll love it."

"I don't really even know what to do, I mean how to start."

"Then it's a lucky thing you've got me along."

With that he leaned over and kissed her — on the mouth, but very gently — then pulled back and looked at her.

"That wasn't so bad, was it?"

"Uh uh."

"And it gets better from here."

This time he kissed her long and hard, and she found herself kissing him back. Afterward, they stayed for a long time with their arms around each other. Her face was pressed into the shoulder of his jacket and she could smell the wet wool mixed up with the scent of his aftershave.

"You park pretty good for someone who's never done it before," he said.

"Maybe I'm just a natural."

"Could be."

She was thinking how much she liked him when he said, "You know, I like you a lot."

"I was just thinking the same thing."

"That you like yourself?"

"That I like you."

"Then it's settled."

"What?"

"That next Friday you'll be ready when I come by to take you to Danburg for the meet. I want you there to cheer me on. Bill'll probably come too, so you'll have someone to sit with and then afterward we can dump him so I can buy you a hamburger and not have to buy him one. He's always broke."

"It's a deal."

"You won't disappear on me again?"

"Promise."

Chapter 9

Kate and Andy made it back about ten minutes before the end of the last act.

"You going back on the bus?" he asked.

"No, with Laura and Bob."

"Okay. I've got to take Bill home . . . so . . . so, I'll see you Friday then. About 7:30."

"Okay."

She went inside and slipped into her seat. When the lights came up, Laura was giving her a powerful fish eye.

"Where've you been?" she asked.

"I ran into an old friend."

Kate knew Laura wouldn't push it while Bob was there, but that there would be a Spanish Inquisition when they got home.

When they got back to Port Williams, Laura and Bob wanted to stop off for a Coke, but Kate begged off. In the first place, she figured they probably wanted to get off by themselves for a while, and in the second place, she wanted to get out from under Laura's fish eye.

And so she talked them into dropping her

off at the house where she intended to go upstairs and practice her eyeliner tricks for next Friday and maybe write her mother. She knew this plan was blown as soon as she got around to the back door and heard all the commotion going on in the kitchen. She didn't know what was happening in there, but whatever it was it was bound to involve Aunt Caroline and was probably going to require some participation from Kate.

Her first thought on coming through the door was that Aunt Caroline had gotten together an animal act. There seemed to be animals everywhere. In fact, there *were* animals everywhere, but when she got a better grip on the situation, she could see that all the hyperactivity — leaping and pouncing and biting and growling and meowing — boiled down to two dogs — a St. Bernard and one that looked not quite like a beagle, but more like a beagle than anything else — and a very small kitten.

Aunt Caroline was at the kitchen counter filling a mixing bowl with crunchies from a ten-pound bag of Woof Chow while the beagle was yapping around her legs and, in periodic fits of frenzy, trying to leap up on the counter. The St. Bernard was standing at her other side with his front paws on the counter, throwing his full body weight against her to nudge her out of the way. The kitten was preoccupied batting back and forth across the linoleum a stray crunchie that had fallen onto the floor.

"Just hold on a minute, boys and girls," Aunt Caroline was saying to the menagerie. "Everybody's going to get dinner."

As she turned to set the bowl on the floor, she saw Kate standing in the doorway. "Oh dear, you gave me a start. I wish you wouldn't skulk in that way."

"I wasn't trying to skulk. I just sort of came in. I guess you didn't hear me because of all the noise."

"Oh. You must wonder what on earth's going on here."

"You robbed a pet store."

"Almost. You know that ASPCA benefit talent show I told you Frank and I were going to tonight? Well, after the show, everyone was invited to visit their facilities. Katie, you just wouldn't believe how many sweet, perfectly wonderful animals they have there. It just broke my heart to think that none of them had homes. And so I told Frank we really ought to pitch in and do our bit."

"Where is Uncle Frank?"

"Well, right now he's down in his workshop. I don't think he's speaking to me at the moment, but I'm sure he'll come around.

You do think they're darling, don't you?"

"Well, sure, but three does sort of seem like a lot at once."

"Not if we divide up the responsibility, I figure. Which one do you want?"

Kate did some fast thinking. "Oh, they're all so wonderful, I don't think I could really pick one over another."

It didn't work. "The kitten, I think. Yes, I think what with your being a quiet sort of person you could probably relate to a cat better than to a dog. What are you going to name it?"

"Gee, I don't know."

"Before that, what are you going to feed it? I stopped at the store and got some dog food, but I forgot to get something for the cat. What do you suppose he'd like?"

"Fish?"

"Maybe there's a can of tuna up in the cupboard. Why don't you take a look."

"I don't see any. What about sardines? Would they be okay?"

"Oh, I'd think so. Why don't you mash some up a little and put them on a plate. I don't think the dogs will try to eat it. I've never heard of dogs liking fish."

Kate set the plate of sardines down on the floor and waited, but the kitten just stayed where he was, a safe distance away in the middle of the doorway leading to the dining room.

"I don't think he's hungry," she told her aunt.

"Well, of course he's hungry. Cats are always hungry, aren't they? He's just scared. After all, he's in a new place and you're a new person and I'm sure he's never seen sardines before. I mean I don't imagine that's what they feed them down at the pound. You'll have to coax him a little."

And so Kate squatted down and put her hand out, and not very imaginatively — but it was all she could think of — started cooing, "Here, kitty, kitty," until it started coming tentatively toward her and the plate.

He was the smallest cat she had ever seen, with light gray fur that tufted out or clumped up in odd places. He looked like a walking handful of dust balls. He came toward her unsteadily, watching her all the time with a look of desperately wanting to trust her, and yet not being quite sure he could. Some where in that long moment of watching him, Kate went over from being a person vaguely interested in cats to a person stuck — for better or worse — with a small, gray kitten.

"I think he likes you," Aunt Caroline said.

"Do you? He probably just wants the sardines."

But when he got to the plate, he just stopped to sniff for a moment, then came over to Kate and started walking around her, brushing up against her ankles and bumping against her, purring so loudly she could hear him even when he was behind her.

"See?" Aunt Caroline said. "He does like you."

"I like him too."

"Why don't you get a bowl of water for him, so he can have a drink if he wants. I made up a litter box for him in the laundry room. He's already used it once, but I don't think it'd hurt to show him where it is again. Then you should probably take him up to your room with you. I was thinking you ought to keep him up there for a while until I get these other beasts under control. If the big one even so much as stepped on him in the middle of the night, it'd be splat."

"Do you know much about what to do with dogs?"

"Oh, sure. Tonight I was going to start teaching them tricks. You know, see if I could get them to leap through a flaming hoop."

"Not really."

"No dear. Not really. I think it's going to be all I can do to keep them from shredding up the living room carpet, and

130

myself awake until Laura comes in. I'm going to try to talk her into taking the St. Bernard. I have to formulate my sales pitch."

"Maybe you could get it to stand very still and tell her you got her a nice, big stuffed animal for her room."

"I was thinking more of using a little parental clout. You know, telling her the dog is hers, or she's grounded until the end of the school year."

Kate went upstairs, holding the kitten in one hand. It couldn't have weighed more than a few ounces. When she got up to her room, she tried to interest him in playing with a piece of ribbon she had, but he was too curious about the attic and set off on his own to explore it by sniffing every square inch.

She lay down on her bed and got back to her Gothic romance, which was to a very good part. The next thing she knew, Laura was waking her up.

"Why do you have all the lights on?"

"I don't know. I was reading. I guess I must've fallen asleep."

"Can you believe this?" she said, pointing to the kitten, which had curled itself into a ball and fallen asleep at the foot of the bed.

"Oh, he's not so bad. I don't think he'll be too much trouble."

"You say that because he is a tiny, winsome kitten, not a full-grown St. Bernard."

"I gather she talked you into dog ownership."

"What could I do? She told me I could take him back tomorrow if I wanted, but that she'd overheard them at the pound saying that because he was so big and hard to find a home for, they were going to have to put him away."

"Maybe you'll get to like him."

"He's already eaten my trigonometry book."

"You were doing lousy in that class anyway."

"The kitten is cute. What did you name him?"

"I don't know. I was thinking of Cardigan. He does look like a little crumpled sweater, doesn't he?"

"Yeah, that's cute. I think I'll call the dog Jaws, in anticipation of him tearing everything in my room to shreds. Now, I'll bet you think the conversion of this house into Bozo's Circusland has distracted me from the many questions I have for you."

"I guess I was sort of hoping."

"Sorry."

"It was Andy. I ran into him in the lobby. We took a ride to talk. So you don't have to take any drastic measures to socially rehabilitate me. I did it all by myself."

"So where do you stand?"

"We're going to the meet Friday night. He'll pick me up so I don't have to go alone."

"Pretty good. Do you think he's interested?"

"I guess. Unless he thinks I'm a needy case and he's just doing it out of the goodness of his heart."

"I doubt that. I mean I know he's interested, but do you think he's *really* interested?"

"Well, if you're going to press me, I guess I might as well tell you. The plans are actually for us to go to the meet on Friday night and then get married on Saturday. Do you think I can find a dress by then?"

"Okay. Okay. Look, don't mind me. I'm just naturally nosy. I'll back off, though."

"Really, Laura. If there were anything to tell, I'd tell you. So far it's not much of anything. When his ship leaves for the Barbary Coast and I decide to hide in a sack of potatoes in steerage to be with him, I'll be sure to let you know my plans."

"What do you think of Bob."

"I like him. A lot. Really."

"He is pretty special, isn't he? Maybe

I should just bag this whole New York idea and hang in with him."

"He'll still be here when you get back."

"Kate, you just know some other girl's going to get her clutches in him before my plane lands in New York."

"Maybe. Do you have gambling blood?"

"I don't know. There haven't been any stakes until now." She stopped and, for a minute, just sat looking full of thought. "I'd better get downstairs."

Although it was after 1:00 when Laura left, Kate felt wide awake, probably because of the nap she had taken with Cardigan. Apparently it hadn't been long enough for him, though. After briefly rallying when Laura came up, he had settled in again on the comforter at the foot of the bed.

It seemed like a good time to write to her mother. She hadn't in two weeks. And so she got out her box of stationery. She liked writing on looseleaf better because then her lines didn't go all crooked, but her mother thought nice stationery "makes a pleasing statement about a person" and so for letters to her mother she always used these little sheets with the script K in the upper left-hand corner.

When she had crumpled up three sheets of false starts, she realized that she was having trouble finding something to say.

It seemed that lately her life was filling up with all sorts of things she wasn't sure her mother would be crazy about. The job at the cleaners. Kate had a strong feeling she would think that was something that would take time away from her studies. The kitten. Her mother had always dismissed pets as "dirty nuisances." And Andy. She wasn't sure on this one, never having had a boyfriend before, but she figured he was something her mother would have a definite opinion on, and just now she didn't really want to find out what that opinion was.

It didn't seem worth risking a showdown over yet. Kate wasn't sure he *was* a boyfriend yet. They hadn't even really had a date. And maybe the kissing hadn't meant anything to him. He couldn't possibly know it was the first time she had ever really been kissed. She would be terribly embarrassed if he knew. He had probably kissed fifty girls. It was probably like shaking hands to him.

But if he had kissed her without caring anything about her, why would he have asked her out? No, even a chronic worrywart like Kate had to admit that as things go, things were looking pretty good.

Chapter 10

One night the next week, Laura told Kate that she was planning to have a show-down with Aunt Caroline and Uncle Frank the next night at dinner.

"About what?" Kate asked.

"I just think it's time we stopped kidding each other about this college thing."

"So you've made up your mind?"

"Well, what I realized the other night is that I'd made up my mind a long time ago. I've just been too scared to tell them. Anyway, I think I'm finally ready to have it out."

"Sounds reasonable."

"Oh, Kate. You're terrific. I knew I could count on you."

"All I said was that it sounds reasonable. What are you counting on me for?"

"To back me up."

"Oh, wait a minute. I'm just the visiting cousin. I don't think it'd be a real good idea for me to get in the middle of something between you and your folks."

"I know. I thought of that. Then I thought how I really don't have anyone else who can give me support, and that you'll just have to do it."

"I guess I see. Look, why don't you do it this way. Start in yourself and see how it goes. Maybe you won't even need me. If you do, I promise I'll back you up."

"You're terrific, Kate."

"I am. I'm superb."

"No. Really."

"Well, try not to put me to the test, will you?"

"You've got a deal."

Dinner that night was a lot more formal. Not in the candelabra and black tie and place card sense. Just in the tone of the conversation.

Laura, who was usually so busy running on at the mouth that Uncle Frank had to shut her up so she would eat, was conspicuously silent in her preoccupation with finding the right moment to plunge in with her sales pitch on New York.

And so the burden of table talk fell on the rest of them, and they weren't doing such a terrific job of it. It struck Kate that they probably sounded like an especially dull TV sitcom family without the benefit of a laugh track to liven things up.

Not that Aunt Caroline wasn't trying.

She asked Uncle Frank how things had gone down at the plant that day, which was good for about a five-second response. Kate's response to how things had gone at school was good for another four seconds.

If Kate had been Laura, she would have given up on the idea of confronting her parents with the New York plan. At least at this particular dinner. The leaden conversation seemed to her a warning about everyone's mood.

Kate almost thought Laura had decided to bag it for the night when finally, in the middle of dessert, she started her argument.

When she was done, it turned out she had more troops on her side than she thought. Aunt Caroline didn't think it was such a bad idea after all.

"I wish you'd told me about it before. Then I wouldn't have gotten so nervous every time you started making noises about not going to college. I was afraid you were planning a career in dry cleaning."

Uncle Frank was a stickier wicket.

"I just can't go along with it," he said. "You know, every paycheck since you were born I've set aside a little something for your education. The way I see it, college is the doorway to opportunity. And here

I've worked hard so you could have this opportunity and now you're talking about not taking advantage of it. Besides, even if you weren't going to college, New York is out of the question. You're too young to go off on your own like that."

"But college would be off on my own."

"It's not the same thing. They keep an eye on you in college. Nobody's going to look out for you in the Big Apple."

"Look at it this way, Frank," Aunt Caroline said. "We won't have to worry about her grades for another four years."

"Caro, those were my last words on the subject. I just won't hear any more about this scheme."

Later that night, Laura came up to see Kate.

"Hey, it went pretty well, didn't it? And I didn't even have to drag you into it."

"What do you mean pretty well? Your dad knocked the idea cold."

"Oh, that's okay. It's my mom who counts. If I keep putting a little pressure on her now and then, she'll probably be able to bring Daddy around."

"It doesn't work that way around my house. My folks are a solid front."

"You just haven't found the chink in their armor."

"Maybe. I guess I haven't had a lot of things that seemed worth bothering to fight for."

"It must be sort of fun — I mean I know it must be lonesome sometimes, but still it must be sort of fun — not having any parents around to nag you for a while."

"Well, my mother still writes every week, and she called Sunday night."

"I didn't know that."

"Yeah, to find out why I hadn't written in two weeks. You know — was I sick, was something wrong that I wasn't telling her? It was a dumb conversation. I wasn't expecting her to call and so I was sort of caught short. You know, in the letters, I have time to drum up stuff to tell her that I think she'll like to hear. On the phone, it's trickier. Like I'll come up with something that seems surefire and I'll get too far into it before I realize there's something about it she'll object to. Sunday night she asked what I'd done that day. Having gone bowling went over fine, but then when I told her about Uncle Frank taking us out to dinner, I knew I'd made a mistake. Not that she'd ever say anything. There's just this little disapproving silence on the other end of the line so I'll pick up on the fact that she's put out and remember that she thinks fast food restaurants are terrible places

140

that serve greasy meals and are hangouts for guys in leather jackets. Stuff like that."

"She never did seem to me like the easiest person to get along with."

"I don't know. It wasn't so bad when I was home. Lately, it's been getting harder. I mean it's not like I've dropped out of school and become a stripper or anything, but there does seem to be a whole lot of stuff going on in my life lately that I'd just rather not go into with her. I think she suspects that and so her letters have been getting more obviously prying and mine have probably been getting more vague. Anyway, things are just a little tense at the moment."

"I think that's one of the ways you know you're growing up."

"What?"

"Well, when the first person you want to tell everything to isn't your mother."

Friday morning Kate got to school about ten minutes late. She had been kept waiting by Laura, who had gotten an outrageously expensive haircut the day before at Salon de Paris and was in the john for over an hour wetting it, then blow-drying it, then rewetting, then reblowing, all the while crying and loudly claiming that she was going to sue Mr. Jacques. She still hadn't emerged by the time Kate finally gave up on her and left. It was already homeroom period by the time she got to her locker and found the note taped to the door.

All it said was, "Don't forget tonight." As if she'd be thinking about anything else all day.

"Aunt Caroline?" Kate called from the kitchen.

"I'm in here."

"Where's here?"

"In the laundry room. I'm just putting some stuff in the dryer."

"Hi."

"Hi."

"You're home early," Kate said.

"Teachers' meetings this afternoon. I snuck off early."

"Oh."

"Something I can do for you?"

"No. I just wanted to let you know I'm going out tonight."

"They're going to put up a plaque for you in that library."

"No, this is fun out."

"Where're you going?"

"To the swim meet."

"I had no idea you were interested in that sort of thing."

"Well, I'm not really. This boy asked me. He'll be coming by."

"Oh my. Then we'll have to do something, won't we. I'll make some lemonade and..."

"No, please don't bother. That's what I wanted to talk to you about."

"About not bothering?"

"Yeah, well, sort of. I just think it'd be neater if it didn't look like this was the biggest thing to happen around here since the color TV was delivered. You know, if you could just treat him like he was one of the million guys who come by every week. Like you would with Laura."

"Oh. I see. Okay, I promise I'll look bored by the whole thing."

"You're terrific, Aunt Caroline."

"If I were terrific, it wouldn't have taken me five minutes to pick up on the point of this conversation. You'd better figure out what you want to wear. From the looks of things around here, everything in this house is unironed."

"I've got some clean jeans and a sweater upstairs. I checked before I left this morning."

This was sort of downplaying it a bit. Actually, Kate had in the past three days tried on practically everything she owned, and changed her mind half a dozen times before arriving at what seemed like the best, if not quite perfect, outfit she had in her closet. Her newest jeans, her navy and green striped sweater, and a white shirt. She still wasn't positive about it, though, and went up to her room to try it on once more before dinner.

After dinner, Kate waited until Laura was done redoing her hair for what seemed like the eightieth time since she had had it cut, then appropriated the bathroom for the next hour. First she took a shower and washed her hair, then blew it dry. Even she had to admit it was looking pretty good since she had it cut on Tuesday afternoon at Bernice's Klip 'n Kurl, which was where Laura used to go before she decided to put herself in the hands of Mr. Jacques at the Salon de Paris. Then she put on some all-over body splash she had bought on the way home from school. It seemed a little overwhelming at first, but then she got used to the scent and figured that it would probably fade some more before she went out, and that the smell of chlorine at the meet would probably overpower it anyway. After that, she cut her toenails and fingernails, put clear polish on both (what the hell, she thought), plucked her eyebrows, and brushed her teeth twice. Then she dumped everything from her make-up box onto the bathroom rug and decided to hold it down to eyeliner, mascara, blusher, and a light peach lipstick for tonight.

When she got back up to her room, she

got dressed and got a surprise looking at herself in the full-length mirror on the inside of the closet door. She didn't ordinarily look at herself at lot. It made her nervous. And so she was pulled up short at what she saw tonight. It wasn't like she didn't recognize herself, or anything that dramatic. But what she saw was certainly a different Kate from what she used to look like and had thought she still looked like. In the first place, it looked like she had dropped about ten pounds. The Meyers didn't have a scale, but she should have guessed that she was losing weight from the way her old clothes had been hanging on her, and from how little of either Laura's or Aunt Caroline's cooking she could bring herself to eat. What she saw wasn't a movie starlet exactly, but a pretty good sixteen-year-old figure now that the last of the baby fat was gone. Also gone were the zits that used to crop up on her chin and forehead. The make-up was just right. It made her a little more sophisticated without looking like she was working at seeming vampy. The new haircut was funky without being outrageous. The only thing definitely wrong were her old glasses. The frames were too small and heavy and out of it and made her look like one of those kids who stayed late every day at school to do independent experiments in the lab.

Maybe she could use some of her cleaners money to get some new ones. Next week. For tonight, though, at least she looked better than she could ever remember looking, and that wasn't nothing.

Andy showed up on time. Aunt Caroline was perfect, passing through the front hall just as Kate was getting her jacket, looking distracted and mildly put out.

"Going out again, Kate? Honestly, I don't know when you get your homework done."

Bill was in the car waiting for them. He got out to let Kate sit in the middle, then slid back in and closed the door after himself.

Andy introduced them.

"Okay, sports fans," Bill said, rubbing his hands together in fake glee, "let's get moving. Got to get over to those bleachers so we can root root root for the home team."

"Is he always this excitable?" Kate asked Andy.

"He's always this much of a nut."

"I gather you're not that crazy about going to this," she said to Bill.

"Not real crazy."

"Then why go?"

"He comes to see me in plays. I watch him swim. Fair's fair. This way we're both

146

equally miserable. Are you a lover of water sports?"

"I'm a curious, impartial observer. I should be able to give you a more solid opinion on swim meets after I've seen one."

"Did you pour on the whole bottle of cologne your sister gave you?" Andy asked Bill without looking over at him. "I can smell you from here."

It was true. The whole car smelled like a combination of lilac water, cloves, and sage. Kate was sort of glad for it, since it was overpowering the body splash she'd gone wild with.

"I guess I did go a little heavy," Bill said. "I probably shouldn't have. It might be dangerous. I mean, even without it, girls are already climbing all over me all the time."

You didn't have to be in on the joke to know he was teasing himself. Bill was about five feet four with what were probably head to toe freckles and a wiry crop of bright red hair that was kinked into permanent pleats. Earlier in the week, looking through Laura's yearbook from last year, Kate saw that he had been voted class clown. There was also a check mark by his picture. She asked Laura what it meant.

"Oh, I was going through the book one

night and thought I'd see how many of the guys in the class I'd gone out with."

"You dated Bill Murphy?"

"I wouldn't say dated. I went out with him once or twice. Everybody does. He's sort of everybody's standby filler. You know, when you're between heavies and you don't want to sit home. Bill runs with the right crowd and so going out with him is a good way to at least get to the parties to see who else is there."

"Isn't that sort of cruel?"

"Cruel how?"

"Well, isn't it sort of using him?"

"I guess. But it's not really cruel. I mean he knows what's going on. He sees that a girl is on the rebound and he asks her out. Is it more cruel for the girl to accept, knowing that it isn't going to develop into anything, or to turn him down?"

"But why do the girls always assume it's not going to develop into anything? Is he so awful?"

"Oh no. Not at all. It's just that he always goes for the coolest girls. He's one of those guys who compulsively dates out of his league. I guess that sounds snobby. But it's just true. It'd be like me only being able to go for the most famous rock stars. I'd just be setting myself up for a broken heart."

Kate found herself once again wondering if sometime after high school the caste system broke down enough so that plain girls could turn into interesting women and attract guys who had a letter sweater up in their attic trunk. And so guys like Bill Murphy could become wildly rich, or successful, or something, and marry a former homecoming queen. She hoped so.

When they got to the school parking lot and out of the car, Andy got almost immediately swept off by a loud bunch of guys carrying athletic bags. He didn't even look back at Kate for a "see you later."

"He has to go in the locker room entrance," Bill told her. "We go around the front."

"Oh."

"Hey. He wasn't brushing us off or anything. It's just that before meets, he gets these acute attacks of star fever. You know. Suddenly it's just him, and the water, and destiny, and we're just the far-off roar of the crowd."

"I think I hate sports."

And so Kate surprised herself by getting caught up in the excitement of the meet. She felt a new kind of rush going through her generated by a bombardment of new sights, and sounds, and smells, and sensations. The bright overhead lights bouncing off the white tile walls and the blue water.

The echo chamber effect that magnified the already frantic cheering of the crowd. The nearly unbearable tension of the swimmers, so visible that it shot into the stands like an electric current, galvanizing the spectators, creating a clench-fisted moment of suspension broken suddenly by the report of the starting gun. And, of course, seeing Andy, looking so strangely lithe in his green nylon tank suit.

By the time Port Williams took the second event, Kate was jumping up and down and hugging Bill in a burst of unconscious spontaneity she wouldn't have thought she had in her.

In the end, Port Williams won and Andy placed first in one of his events and second in the other. She expected him to be elated afterward, but when she met him in the hall outside the showers, he seemed oddly down.

Bill slapped him on the back. "Way to go."

"Yeah, yeah."

"Say. I ran into Rudy at the Coke stand. We're going to buzz by that party at Linda Schwartz's. You two want to come along?"

Kate hoped he would say yes. Linda Schwartz was solid cool. Everybody was bound to be at her party. It was a chance she never had back in Springville, to be — at least for a night — on the inside of what was going on instead of off with the outer fringe of spectators.

"No thanks, man. I promised Kate a hamburger. I'll just see you on Sunday, okay? Eddie's dad just got a new color TV. He's hot for us to come watch the basketball game with him."

"Okay by me. See you then. See you, Kate."

"Yeah. See you, Bill."

She turned back to Andy. "You didn't have to bag the party on my account. I would've gone."

"Aw, it's just going to be the same old crowd. And Linda's folks are big on hanging around. I'd rather go get a hamburger and talk. Or a pizza. Yeah, what about Luigi's?"

"Okay by me."

"You hungry?"

"Not too."

"Then you probably don't want to go to Luigi's."

"Are you? Hungry?"

"Starved."

"Then let's go. You order a pizza and I'll have some."

After he ordered, she told him she thought it had been a terrific meet.

"The best you've ever been to, eh?"

"Well, I know I don't have a lot to com-

151

pare it to — to be exact, nothing — but still, I got real excited there a couple of times. And I don't get excited a lot."

"Glad you had a good time."

"You looked very good in there. Especially in the 100-meter."

"Let's not talk about it, okay?"

"I though that's why we came here. To have a pizza and talk, you said."

"Sure, let's talk. Just not about that. I don't like losing and I especially don't like talking about losing."

"But the worst you did was come in second."

"Second is not first, so it's losing."

"Aren't you being sort of hard on yourself?"

"Maybe, but that's my business, isn't it?"

"Sure. Sorry."

"Hey, forget it. I don't want to ruin the whole night. Let's talk about you. Like how'd your week go?"

"My cat got an ear infection."

"I think I'd rather talk about losing."

They both laughed and, for the rest of the night, it was okay between them.

She wound up eating half of his pizza. Sometimes, especially when Laura did the cooking, Kate spent most of the meal trying to push the food around on her plate and smash it down into the smallest possible piles to make it look as if she had eaten something. Tonight Laura had fixed a combination Waldorf-macaroni salad with honey mayonnaise dressing. She was also into vegetable desserts at the moment and, after having had some success with a carrot cake last week, pushed it too far tonight with a batch of tomato chip cookies. So Kate had finished dinner feeling about as hungry as when she started, but she had been so nervous getting ready, and then so distracted at the meet that she hadn't noticed until the waitress set the hot, juicy, delicious (just as the menu described it) pizza on the table.

"Sorry I brought you here tonight," Andy said. "I mean seeing that you weren't hungry."

"I guess I was but didn't know it." She told him about the cooking situation at the Meyers'.

"It's hard to imagine Laura Meyers cooking at all. I mean it's hard to imagine her doing anything besides sitting there looking lost in class, or standing there looking good at a party. But then I have a lot of trouble that way — imagining people out of the contexts where I see them."

"I'm just the opposite. I'm always making up whole life stories for people I just see on the bus."

153

"Are you sort of getting to notice that you and I are different in a whole lot of different ways."

"I guess we are."

"Do you think that's good?"

"I don't think it's bad."

"I think it's good."

"Good."

"I figure I might learn something new from you. I'm always hanging around with people who are almost exactly like me. They say something and I've already just thought it. No surprises, you know."

"You talk like I'm a Martian."

"Oh no. What I was thinking is that you're just different enough. Too different is another thing. Like Vivian Carswell. I took her out once and she spent about half an hour talking about Tolstoy before I figured out he was a writer. I thought he was a general."

"Nope. He's a writer."

"You knew that?"

"Yeah, but I wouldn't talk about him for half an hour."

"That's what I mean. You're different, but not so wound up in being different that you have to go around talking about it all the time. I think I like you."

"I think you said that before."

"Yeah, but now I'm more sure. Right

now I'd say I'm right between thinking I like you and being sure I like you."

"With me it's that I think I'm sure I like you, but I'm not quite sure."

"You're pulling my leg, aren't you?"

"A little."

"Watch it. I've got very sensitive legs."

Chapter 11

"Hey guess what?" Laura shouted to Kate from across the length of the attic, out of breath from running up the stairs two at a time. So many of their conversations started this way that Kate had begun to think of herself as a rock and Laura as a crashing wave that descended upon her from time to time. For the most part she didn't mind these interruptions, but at this particular moment she was reluctant to be torn away from her book.

"What?" she said, sighing as she turned down a corner of the page and closed the book.

"I won. Daddy gave in. If I can save up enough money, I can go to New York and give it a try."

"Hey, that's great. It wasn't even that hard, was it?"

"That's true, isn't it? And to think of all the time I spent worrying about it. I should've had it out with them months ago."

"Months ago you weren't sure this was what you wanted to do."

"I guess. Anyway, now I've got to start planning. I've been figuring up my high finances and with what I've got in the bank now, plus what I can make at the cleaners before June, plus what I can get from a better job during the summer, I should be able to leave in the fall. And if I could get a waitressing job out at the country club, I could probably make a lot more — with tips and all — than at the cleaners. All I really need is enough to last maybe two or three months out there without a job. Then, if I'm not starring in a long-running Broadway hit by November, I can probably get a waitress job or something to keep body and soul together, and look for parts, and take acting lessons during the day. Daddy'll foot the bill for the lessons. He says he's already got the money put away for my higher education and it looks like this is going to be it."

"That's quite a turnaround for him."

"Not so drastic. I think he thinks I'm going to be home in six months with my tail between my legs, ready to straighten up and go to college like a sensible girl."

"What do you think?"

"I think I'm going to be a star."

"That isn't terribly realistic, is it?"

"Kate, I'm giving up my whole life here,

everything I know, and putting it all on a longshot. I don't think I can afford to be realistic."

"But you would come back if things turned out badly? You wouldn't stay ten years just to prove a point?"

"People do that, you know. All the time. But no, I don't think I'm made of that kind of stuff. Like I told you, I think I could only take being kicked around for a year at the most. Will you come and visit me? I'll have a real apartment of my own and everything, probably. We could go out to dinner, and to some plays, and to Greenwich Village. Your mother wouldn't let you, would she?"

"I don't know. I could lie a little and say you were staying in a girls' dormitory."

"That's a pretty well-developed lie. Did you just think it up right now?"

"Yeah. I guess my mind works pretty well on the subject of how to get around my mother. What about Bob? Have you told him?"

"Are you crazy? Why would I have told him before I was sure my parents would go along with it? Just to throw fat on the fire? Get a good running argument going? I guess I'll have to talk to him about it pretty soon, though. I dread that worse than telling my folks. He won't be mad; he'll just get all hurt looking and mope around until I leave, like I've got some terminal disease."

"Maybe he'll just dump you fast for Alice Ann Crouse."

"What a thing to say!"

"Just a tweak. You did sound a little conceited, assuming your going away is going to be the end of the world for him."

"I guess maybe I did sound a little smug. But I still think he's going to be crushed. How's your romance going?"

"Oh. I guess I haven't really started thinking of it as a romance yet. I think it's fine. As of last night anyway."

"Did you have a good time?"

"I guess I could be cool about it and just say, 'Yeah, it was okay,' but I guess I don't have to be cool with you. It was so much fun, Laura. I think maybe it was the best single time I've ever had. He's not perfect — like he gets mad real quick at stuff you can't predict he'll get mad at, and sometimes he's not all that quick on the uptake — but he's a lot of fun, real easy to talk to and kid around with and stuff. And he really likes me. I can tell. The other thing — I know this isn't the most mature reason for liking somebody, but I can't help it — is that he is *so* cute."

"Cute he is all right. What'd you do last night? After the meet, I mean. There was a big party at Linda Schwartz's. I sort of expected you'd turn up there."

"He didn't want to go. We went for a pizza instead."

"You got in kind of late."

"It wasn't much past 1:00. I didn't see your light on, so I thought you were still out."

"Bob was going ice fishing with his dad at 5:30 this morning, so he wanted to get to bed early. Where'd you go? Luigi's?"

"Yeah."

"I thought that closed at midnight."

"Laura. Are you interrogating me?"

"I guess I am, sort of."

"We went up to the bluff for a while."

"Kate, I hate to sound like your mother, but I know you don't have a whole lot of experience and well, well it'd make me feel better if you told me you've got everything under control. I mean this is a really small town and all the guys kiss and tell."

"Well, if he's telling, all he's got to tell is kissing."

"That takes a load off my mind."

"What'd you think?"

"Oh nothing in particular. I just wanted to make sure you knew this was a place where a girl can still get a reputation. And for hardly anything. Were you reading when I came up?"

"Yeah."

"You always get up this early on Saturday? I thought I'd have to drag you out of bed and over to the cleaners."

"I don't know why — usually I sleep until the last minute — but I got up at 7:00 this morning. It's almost time to go, isn't it?" she said, stretching to reach under the bed for her alarm clock. "Yep."

"I'll go get dressed," Laura said. "Meet you downstairs in twenty minutes?"

"Okay."

Late in the afternoon, during a slack period between the bursts of customers who had been coming in all day, Laura's friend Karen stopped by.

"I just got the most darling shirt and pair of slacks at Harman's," she told Laura, and started to open up the bag to show her.

"You can't do this, Karen," Laura told her. "I told you how Gomez hates it if friends come by here. 'Personal visitors' he calls them. Bob already stopped by this morning. If Gomez comes up front and sees me fooling around with you, it'll probably be the end of my career in cleaning."

"Don't sweat it. If he comes out, I'll just pretend I'm bringing the stuff in to be pressed. He won't come up front, will he?"

"Probably not. I think he's back in the office getting depressed over the cost of hangers and plastic bags. So show me what you got." And then to Kate, "Come see too."

"Hi, Kate."

"Hi."

"Well. What do you guys think?"

It really was a spectacular outfit — the shirt striped in three or four colors of green, one of which exactly matched the bottle green of the slacks — and started Kate figuring how much longer she would have to save before she could start reminding Aunt Caroline about the shopping trip to Chicago.

"It's really a terrific outfit, Karen," Kate said.

"Did they come together?" Laura asked.

"Two separate departments, can you believe it?"

"Incredible. Now you've got to find someplace good enough to wear it."

"Well, that's the thing. It got me to thinking, why don't I have a party. Actually, that wasn't quite the order of my thinking. The first thing was my parents going to Miami on Saturday. The second thing was party. The third thing was getting something terrific to wear. So what do you think?"

"I think your folks'll find out."

"So I probably shouldn't do it?"

"So you should for sure tell everybody you invite that it's a top secret number and that everyone should say they're going to the show."

"You're so smart. I guess I'll have to invite you two now that you're in on the plot."

"Cripes, here comes Gomez. I can hear him whistling. That means it's time to count the cash in the register. You'd better buzz out of here, Karen, before you have to spend half of your allowance getting those things pressed."

"Is she really going to do it, do you think? Give the party?" Kate asked Laura as they were walking home from the cleaners.

"I guess."

"Do you think I should come?"

"Sure. Why not? She invited you, didn't she?"

"Are you going?"

"I guess."

"But with Bob."

"Probably."

"But who will I go with?"

"Come with us. He won't mind giving you a lift. He likes you, you know."

"He does?"

"Yeah. He told me a couple of times. He thinks you're funny."

"About the party. Don't I have to come with someone? You know, with a date or something?"

"Oh no. I just said I'd be going with Bob because I usually do. You're not going steady with anybody so it's fine for you to come by yourself. If I weren't going with Bob, I'd just come alone. Parties around here are kind of loose that way."

"I don't think I have anything to wear."

"Of course you do. This isn't a coronation ball. It's just a bunch of the kids getting together at Karen's. Just wear jeans. What are you so nervous about anyway?"

"I don't know. Nothing, I guess. Anything new makes me nervous."

"Would you stop sounding like a dip. The way you talk about yourself, you'd think you were the biggest twinkie ever to hit the planet. Then, after all your worrying, you get into a situation and you're just fine. Really, I think the only person who thinks you're out of it is you."

"You think?"

"What do you think — I'm lying?"

"I guess not. I don't know. I mean I know you're not lying, but it's just a little hard to see it that way from inside me."

"Is inside you a hard place to be?".

"Yeah, sort of."

"I thought so. Inside me is no picnic either sometimes. It must be the same for everybody."

"Do you think you ever get beyond that,

past feeling nervous and worried about so much stuff? Sometimes I've thought that must be where being an adult gets you — beyond all this."

"It'd be nice, wouldn't it? I've got a feeling, though, that growing up is just shifting into a new set of worries. You know, money, and kids, and growing old."

"Well, that cheers me up, knowing that I've got a whole set of replacement worries ahead of me."

"These are the best years of your life, Katie."

"You're only young once."

"Ten years from now you'll laugh at this."

"*That* one I've never bought."

"Well, I can tell you this for sure. Ten years from now, you won't even remember what you wore to Karen Munson's party."

Kate did wear jeans after all. And she did go with Laura and Bob.

They got there early to help Karen straighten up the place and put together some cheese and crackers and stuff.

"I don't think you really have to do all this," Laura told Karen when they started to work in the kitchen. Bob was off getting a couple of bags of ice to throw in the washtubs in the basement for the pop and beer everybody would bring.

"I know," Karen said. "I just wanted to make something different from chips and dips. Do you think cheese and crackers is too hoity toity?"

"No, it'll be cute," Laura said. "I just wouldn't go as far as cucumber sandwiches."

Bob came back with the ice, then went up to watch the basketball game on the TV in Karen's parents' room. The girls finished putting out the goodies, then sat down in the family room to wait for people to show up. Kate mostly listened while Laura and Karen gossiped outrageously about what seemed to be everyone in the senior class, making Kate all the gladder that she had kept her mouth shut about Andy. It was sort of fun sitting around listening to them speculate about why Nancy Weller and Todd Michaels were getting married next month instead of after graduation, and how much Liz Wyeth's nose job had cost.

Then Karen turned to her and said, "Laura tells me you're going out with Andy Chase these days." The way she said it, Kate could tell she wasn't looking for a one-word response, but she tried anyway.

"Yeah."

"Is it a heavy deal?"

"Naw, I've just seen him a couple of times."

"I asked him to come tonight."

"Oh. Good." Kate tried to speak in as flat and uninterested a monotone as she could work up and just hoped she wasn't turning red, or perspiring, or doing anything dopey that would give her away.

"This girl's one cool customer, Laura," Karen said. "I think we'll have to get out the rack and torture the information out of her."

"Really. There's nothing to tell."

"Except that you're crazy about each other and about to run off together next weekend. You're no fun at all, Kate. Come on, give a couple of dirt-diggers a break. Andy Chase is a big mystery man around here. You can help us crack his mystique."

"I don't know much about his mystique," Kate said, unable to resist sounding a little smug. "I only know about him. So far he seems pretty terrific. At least to me."

"Terrific, eh? You think it's going to turn into something? You and him?"

"I don't know. Maybe a medium-sized something."

Just then the buzzer went off and Kate thought it was probably the first time in her life she had actually been saved by the bell.

After waiting for what seemed like an awfully long time for anybody to show up, about fifty kids came within the next twenty minutes. A lot of them brought records and all of them brought stuff to drink. Some of the guys were over eighteen and brought beer.

Within an hour everybody was dancing, or making out on the couches in the darkened family room, or just fooling around acting drunker than they were, considering that there were maybe four six-packs to go around. Kate hung around on the edge of things until a tall, sort of pasty-looking guy named Dave Kruger asked her if she wanted to dance, which she did for a couple of numbers, then sat out a few more, sipping a beer with him. It was the first time she had ever tasted beer, and was disappointed to find that it didn't make her feel wildly high. At first she thought it might be the beer that was making her sleepy, but soon after figured out that it was more likely Dave Kruger's boring preoccupation with rock electronics. Apparently he was into building synthesizers, and mixing equipment and the like, and assumed an equally rabid interest on her part.

She could have gotten away from him easily enough by saying she had to go and help Karen out with something, but she stayed. For one thing, it kept her safely on the sidelines. The momentum of the party was beginning to frighten her a bit. She didn't think she was good enough to get out and dance as well as the other kids, and even if she had someone she wanted to make out with, she certainly wouldn't want to do it on one of the couches in full view of everybody else, and she couldn't see herself just jumping into the snowball fight that had started up in the back yard.

The other thing was that it was sort of a new pleasant feeling, being bored by Dave Kruger, letting him drone on and on without caring what he might think about her, without being nervous about coming up with interesting things to say. Maybe Laura was right about her. Maybe she just thought she was a turkey and so let it get her all clenched up. For sure, if she could be as loose around everybody as she was around Dave Kruger, a lot of her problems would disappear.

Unfortunately, this confidence-building reverie was instantly shattered by the confidence-shattering entrance into the family room of Andy, his arm draped over the shoulders of Kim Thomas.

If the potted palm behind her had been big enough, she would have slunk behind it and hid there until everyone had left. Why had she let herself tell Laura and Karen that there was something between her and him. She would have given anything to have gone back to letting everybody think she didn't have a boyfriend. Much worse was talking like she had one, only to have him show up an hour later latched onto Kim Thomas.

And it would have to be Kim Thomas — the dopiest girl in her history class. Probably the dopiest girl in the entire junior class. Kim Thomas wouldn't know which end of her pencil to write with and probably never would've been let beyond second grade if she hadn't been so cute that all the guys in every class she had had always been willing to write her papers for her and let her crib their answers on tests. Kim Thomas — the class ding-a-ling who Kate had convinced herself would only attract the dopiest guys. It just couldn't be worse.

Maybe, she thought — while nodding at what she thought were appropriate places in Dave Kruger's conversation about setting up recording acoustics in a basement — maybe Andy and Kim just lived on the same block or something and he offered her a lift to the party. This hope rapidly dematerialized when she next looked over and saw them on one of the couches looking like they were welded together, nuzzling and kissing and laughing intermittently at what appeared to be very private jokes.

After about ten minutes of trying to think of a way out of this mess, she gave up and interrupted Dave Kruger in his monolog.

"What do you say we get out of here so we can be alone for a while."

She couldn't believe she was saying it, but what else could she do? Dave Kruger was her only possible escape from hanging around and enduring this humiliation for as long as it took for the party to break up. At least by leaving with him, she could salvage a few shreds of dignity by making it seem like she, too, was interested in somebody new.

"Well," Dave Kruger said. "Like where would you want to go?"

"I'll leave it to you. I know you'll be able to think of something."

Not too surprisingly, he thought of the bluff. Somebody probably mentioned it to him once while he was testing the circuits on his moog.

It was a chancy move, but she lucked out. By acting real interested and keeping him talking about what brands of equipment various bands used, she kept the physical aspect of their half hour out on the bluff down to one short, nervous kiss, after which she immediately backed off and faked a shiver.

"Sure is cold out here."

"I can start the car up and turn on the heater."

"Better not. We might die of carbon monoxide."

"Is that possible when you're outdoors?"

"Well, I wouldn't want to take any chances with it. I have to be in pretty soon anyway."

"It's only 11:00."

"Is it that late? Then we'd really better hurry. My aunt's real strict."

"Does Laura have to be in at 11:00?"

"Well, she's seventeen. Once I turn seventeen, my aunt says all the rules will be off."

"When will that be?"

"Oh, not for a few months yet."

"You want to go out sometime? We could start early so you could be in on time."

"Oh sure. Just give me a call."

"What about next Friday?"

"Sure. Oh, wait. Friday night I have to take my kitten in for his shots."

"Oh."

"But call me sometime."

"Maybe you'd like to come over and take a look at my equipment."

"That'd be terrific."

She talked him into just letting her off in front of the house and let herself in the front door, hoping to get upstairs and be long asleep by the time Laura came home and decided Kate probably needed a late-night sympathy session.

She hadn't counted on Aunt Caroline being in the living room, on the floor, doing a jigsaw puzzle.

"Hiya, Katie."

"Hi. Good night."

"What do you mean, 'Hi. Good night'?"

"Well, I'm a little tired. I thought I'd just go up to bed."

"Oh. Do you think you could spare just a minute to help me find where this piece of sky goes? There're about one hundred fifty sky pieces — all exactly the same color blue."

"I'm lousy at jigsaw puzzles."

"You've got to be better than someone who's been looking at this stupid puzzle for the past two and a half hours. Come on. Be a sport."

"Okay. But I really don't think I'm going to be much help."

Kate took off her coat, threw it on the chair closest at hand, and sat down on the floor next to Aunt Caroline.

"It doesn't look like you're making much progress," Kate said after she looked over the puzzle. "There still seem to be about one hundred forty-five sky pieces left."

"Oh, I haven't been working on the sky part. I thought I'd save that for when you came home. But look at how far I've gotten on the picket fence. Did you have a good time at the movies?"

Kate almost said "What movie?" before she caught herself and said, "It was okay."

"Which one did you go see?"

"The spy thing over at the Rialto."

"I thought you already saw that one."

"Yeah, but Laura and Bob hadn't seen it and they wanted to go and so I went along and saw it again."

"Where are they?"

"I guess they went out for something to eat. I wasn't hungry."

"So they dropped you off?"

"No, we ran into a guy from school. Dave Kruger. He brought me home."

"You don't look like you had a terrific time."

"It was okay."

"I'd say you look like it was worse than okay."

"Well, we ran into another guy there. Not the one I came home with. The one I went out with the other night. He was with another girl."

"Ah. Well, that's a stinger all right."

"Yeah, well, what do you do about it?"

"If it's that you're crazy about him, you

could think of going after him tooth and nail, fighting her to the death over him. If it's more just the indignity of watching him show up with somebody else, I'd think the best thing would probably be to just swallow your pride and forget it."

"Well, forgetting it would be the smart thing in this case, I guess. It just seems a little hard to do at the moment."

"What's this piece of picket fence doing still in the box here? I thought I had that all put together. Unless this piece is really part of the steeple. You know, if it's any consolation — and it never is, I know — this sort of thing happens to everybody all the time. It may even happen to you a dozen more times. And you'll probably dump on a dozen guys yourself. It's all part of the sorting out process everybody has to go through. Well, not quite everybody. But I think the ones who don't — the girls who marry the first guy who comes along — well, they're more to pity usually.

"See if you can detach yourself from this thing tonight for a minute and look at it academically, or scientifically. Like through a microscope or telescope. This whole dating thing — aside from being mostly fun — is all leading up to people matching up and pairing off and getting married. To be married to somebody for fifty years or so, you've got to really like him. Believe me. To know who you do like, you have to be able to compare and contrast him with who you don't like. The only way to build up this kind of backlog of experience is to go with a lot of fellows. And to go with a lot of fellows — unless you're an extremely agile juggler and can collect thirty or forty guys and like them all equally and keep them all happy simultaneously — you're going to have to break off with a lot of fellows. And that means some pain along the way. Tonight was just one bad shuffle of the cards. There'll probably be more. Mixed in with some good ones. And hopefully it'll all come out right in the end."

"I don't think I could take this happening thirty or forty more times."

"Well, it's not always going to happen like this. Sometimes it'll be you who loses interest or finds someone else. Sometimes you'll both just sort of drift off."

"But what if I do fall for thirty or forty more guys and every one of them dumps on me?"

"Then you might have a real problem and we can talk about it some more. But it's not going to happen that way. I promise."

"Aunt Caroline, I think about half these

sky pieces you have here belong to the pond."

"Now why would they make a puzzle with the sky and the pond exactly the same color? I hope they don't use this puzzle in insane asylum recreation rooms. It could drive some poor nut over the brink."

"I think I'll leave you to it. I'll help you more tomorrow if you want, but I'm really pretty tired now."

"Okay. I think I'll just work on it until Laura gets in."

"Say. Could you not mention what we were talking about to her. I'm not too crazy about spreading it around."

"Oh. Sure."

Upstairs in bed, with Cardigan snuggled asleep in the hollow behind her bent knees, Kate lay thinking about how Aunt Caroline was probably right. And then about how easy it was for her to be right, being twenty years beyond all this with a husband, house, and career, and everything long ago settled for her. And how little good knowing Aunt Caroline was right did Kate, who still had so many hard parts ahead of her.

Chapter 12

One of the two things Kate figured she could count on for sure was that Laura would have plenty to say to her on the subject of Andy, Kim Thomas, the party, and how Kate had handled the situation (probably hopelessly wrong).

The other thing was that she would never hear from Andy again. It made her sad to think that her first romance had fizzled out before it had ever really flared. And that it had fizzled in such an embarrassingly public way. (Actually, only Laura and Karen knew, but that was public enough for her.)

And so she was first surprised when all Laura said — as they were doing the breakfast dishes Sunday — was, "Tough luck about Andy. Don't let it get you too down, though. Kim has swooped down on the best of us. The girl's a real scavenger."

The second surprise came on Tuesday morning when Andy was waiting by her locker when she came in.

"Hi."

"Hi."

"I thought you might want to go to the show."

"Thanks, but I've got to be in homeroom in five minutes."

"Smarty. Okay, what about Saturday night? Would that be more convenient?"

"What's playing?"

"I don't know. Does it matter?"

"Well, maybe it's something I've already seen and hated."

"Are you being deliberately difficult?"

"A little."

"Two can play that game, you know. I think I'll just be difficult and say if you want to take the chance and come, fine. If not, we can just forget it."

"It sounds like it's worth the risk. If it's *The Creature from the Quicksand Pit* I can alway nap through it."

"You teed off about something? About me not saying hi at the party? You know, I tried to get over and talk to you, but I got sort of tied up."

"That's okay."

"You looked sort of tied up yourself."

"Not really."

"Well, you looked pretty tight with Kruger when you two took off."

"I'm not tight with Dave Kruger."

"I think he thinks he's tight with you. I

179

heard him yesterday talking by the gym lockers."

"Oh."

"So. You want to check with him before you let me know for sure about Saturday night?"

"Will you get out of here. I'll see you Saturday. What time?"

"I don't know. I'll check the show times and call you in the afternoon."

"Okay."

Until now, Kate had thought dating was going to be an end to lots of her problems. Maybe it was only the beginning of a whole new set of them. She hadn't even thought of the possibility that it was going to be all this complicated, what with her liking Andy, and him liking Kim Thomas, but apparently liking her too, and not seeming to think there was anything complicated about that. And Dave Kruger, who she couldn't care less about, liking her just fine and apparently telling everyone that he did, and maybe that she liked him too. And Andy thinking she liked Dave Kruger. Or maybe he was just trying to put her on the defensive. She really wasn't prepared to deal with all this at once. And so soon.

For the next couple of months, it kept on going like this. Things didn't get any less complicated, but eventually Kate got used to never being quite sure what was going to happen next.

Andy would ask her out, sometimes for two weekends in a row, then she would hear about or see him going around with someone else (usually, but not always, Kim Thomas). Apparently this was the way he operated and there really wasn't much she could do about it. Or if there was, she never got to a point where she was sure enough of her own feelings to do it. She bounced constantly back and forth on the matter. One minute she was sure she must be in love with him. Then she would wonder if she wasn't just in love with the idea of being in love.

He found out that she liked chocolate raisins and started bringing a bag of them along whenever they went out. She was never sure whether it was the raisins she liked, or him for being sweet enough to remember, or just the fact that someone liked her well enough to make the gesture.

Other times — usually after a night out when he had missed three of her jokes in a row, or had talked for twenty minutes about a dumb water fight the guys had had in the locker room like it was the funniest thing that had happened since Vaudeville died, or had acted real self-important about what a hotshot swimmer he was — she would lapse for a while into not liking him much at all. Then if he called to ask her out for the next weekend, she would think maybe she was being too fussy about him and say okay. If he didn't call for a week or two, she would sink into such a state of despair over the possibility that he might never call again, that she began thinking again that she must be in love with him.

Then there was the problem with Dave Kruger. Actually, it hadn't really become a problem yet, just something she didn't quite know what to do about. Fortunately, he always called at the last minute — usually on Thursday or Friday — long after she had given up on Andy for that weekend. And so if she didn't have anything planned, she would say yes and go out with him. She just couldn't bring herself to make up something like that she was going to be washing her hair, or any of the five or six other polite lies Laura had told her would eventually get rid of any bothersome guy. And Dave Kruger wasn't really bothersome so much as he was just boring.

Kate couldn't pin down precisely what made him so boring. When he got off electronic music, which was pretty much of the time now that he had figured out that the subject put her into a coma, he tried really hard to find common interests and bring up interesting topics. But the fact was that, no matter what the topic, Dave Kruger could find a way to be boring about it.

Still, she figured going out with him was good experience for all the boring guys she would probably wind up dating in her future life. Then she would have periodic bouts of self-recrimination about the whole thing when she stopped to think that going out with Dave Kruger because he provided her with practice in being bored probably wasn't being very nice to him.

And so, through Andy and Dave Kruger and sometimes through Laura, Kate found herself at least on the edges of what social life there was around Port Williams High. That is, she never really got invited anywhere by herself, but if Andy brought her to a party, or Dave Kruger brought her along to the McDonald's with a gang of kids after the show or a basketball game, or if Laura brought her along to the shopping center after school with Karen and her other friends, nobody seemed to mind.

And around school, everyone had started to at least acknowledge her presence. They'd say, "Hiya, Kate" or "How's it going, Kate?" when they passed her in the halls, or ask her how she thought she did on a test.

What didn't happen was getting asked to sit with anybody at lunch, or go out after school with anybody for a Coke. Even Dave Kruger and Andy weren't much help during the week. Dave went around in a fog of academic seriousness. Instead of lunch, he took an extra study hall and he stayed in the library until 4:00 or 5:00 every day. He was hell-bent on becoming a Merit Scholar. With Andy, it was something else. From the very casual hellos she got from him during change of classes, usually followed up by little or no conversation, Kate picked up on the fact that he wanted to keep things cool between them — at least in public. It wasn't exactly that she was the secret woman in some hidden pocket of his life. He did occasionally bring her to parties and stuff. But for some reason, he apparently wanted other people to think things were much more casual between him and Kate than he wanted her to think, given a lot of the things he said to her when they were parked out on the bluff. It wasn't a situation that thrilled her, but on the other hand, it didn't bother her all that much. Most of the time.

And Laura was too wrapped up in herself to give Kate a whole lot of attention. They still had their late-night talk sessions a couple of times a week, and fooled around a lot at the cleaners on Saturdays whenever Gomez disappeared, but around school Kate hardly ever saw her. Even in the drama club, Laura was usually out front rehearsing and Kate was always backstage painting scenery, or mimeographing programs, or hemming costumes.

Actually, Kate had made a couple of friends in the drama club. All on her own too. Molly and Emma Evans. They were backstage lackeys like Kate and the three of them wound up on a lot of odd jobs together through the months of getting ready for *The Little Foxes*. The good things about Molly and Emma were that they were smart and funny and into books like Kate was. After a while, they got a trade-off going with their paperbacks, which saved them all money and got them reading the same books so they could talk about them. The bad things about Molly and Emma were that they were twins and so shared a lot of dippy in-jokes that had probably been going on between them since they were born. And that they were sophomores, which meant they had different classes and a different lunch period from Kate, and so she didn't get to see much of them outside of drama club. A couple of times, she tried to make plans with them to do something out of school, but they were baby-sitting the first time and working on a new set of matching outfits the other time. After that, Kate waited to see if they would ask her to do something with them. When they didn't, she felt a little sad, but then figured that, maybe if you had a twin, you just didn't need to go around looking for other people to do stuff with.

From time to time, she missed the easy camaraderie of her old crowd back home. After the first few weeks she was in Port Williams, when she got three letters from Lucy, Kate didn't hear from her again until the end of April. As soon as Kate saw the return address on the letter lying on the coffee table, she knew Lucy must have some hot news. She took the letter upstairs to her room, flopped down on her bed, ripped it open, crumbled up the envelope and tossed it across the room for Cardigan to chase and bat around, and settled in to read:

Dear Kate,
   I know I am a rotten letter-writing friend, but I have to say that for a long time, there really wasn't much happening to write about. Now there is all sorts of stuff going on here and so I'm hoping you'll forgive me and pretend like there hasn't been so much time between this letter and the one before it.
   The first thing is that Norma won third place in the all-city Science Fair.

She won it for a transparent model of the circulatory system of the frog. I guess she deserved some sort of prize. She's been working on the dumb thing for three months and her mother nearly killed her after all the fake blood leaked out one night all over the new wall-to-wall carpeting.

Nothing is new with Bootsie. Nothing ever is with her. Oh, except she got two turtles for her birthday and tells us she is teaching them tricks. Sometimes you just have to walk away from her because there's nothing you can say.

Andrea — and this is news I think you'll agree — has got a real live boyfriend, if you can imagine Jack Watson as anybody's boyfriend. All we hear about now is Jack, Jack, Jack. She even refers to his acne as "his hormonal imbalance," and calls him Jackson and bought him a cashmere sweater for his birthday, which is probably the only thing he owns that isn't covered with soup stains. He writes her poems (all terrible — she shows us) and they're together all the time and even blow kisses at each other during change of classes. Really, it's enough to make you lose your lunch.

Just so you won't think this is sour

grapes, I should tell you that I've been going with Eddie Mercer lately. Now before you start moaning "Oh no, not Eddie Mercer," I want you to know he's got a whole lot cooler since you left. He stopped wearing the same pair of green corduroy pants and stopped letting his mother cut his hair. I mean I know he's not Bruce Jenner or anything, but he is sort of cute in his own way, don't you think? Well, anyway, I do.

By "going together" I mean we have had five dates five weekends in a row. I think he is going to work up the nerve to kiss me good night by next Saturday. But then I've thought this for the past two Saturdays. So far, we get to the door and I close my eyes and let my lips go as mushy and appealing looking as I can and then I feel him shaking my hand. Oh well. I don't suppose you have any kissing tips, but if you do, maybe you could write me.

The other things about him are all better than his kissing (or should I say non-kissing?). He is real funny for one thing. Cracks me up all the time. And he's interested in my music. He came to the concert two weeks ago and sat right in the second row.

Other than this news, everything else has been extremely dull around here and it'll be fun to have you back this summer although you'll probably have a lot of catching up to do what with most of us getting so boy crazy this year.

This was signed, "Your pal, Lucy."

Kate had to laugh at the notion that she would have to catch up with Lucy, who was still getting handshakes at the door.

Getting Lucy's letter was the first thing in a long time that made Kate think about going back to Springville. And rolling over on her bed and looking out the open attic window down at the budding tree in the front yard, she realized that going back wasn't all that far off anymore. A few months ago, she would have been overjoyed at this. Now, her feelings were mixed. Of course she missed her mom and dad and Lucy and their house and her old room. But so many things had changed for her since she left. Springville seemed like a place from her past. It was sort of hard imagining going back to the way she was and the life she led there. With all her mother's rules that she didn't have to fol-low here. Without Andy. Maybe without a job and all the extra money she was used to having. Maybe without Cardigan. She just didn't know if her parents would approve of either a job or a cat.

After a couple of days of brooding about all this, she decided to talk to Aunt Caroline — about how she thought Kate's mother would react to some of the surprises Kate had in store. Kate waited until she got home from school on Tuesday and then until Aunt Caroline went down to the basement to work out on her exercycle — always a good time to corner Aunt Caroline as she was bored to death on the exercycle and would talk about anything for the fifteen minutes she was stuck on it.

"I don't know, Katie. I think I may have even mentioned your job to your mother when I wrote her last month. Maybe she already knows about that much at least."

"I don't think so. If she knew about it, I would have heard about it by now."

"Well, so what if she doesn't know yet. I don't see that anything you're springing on her is such a big deal. So you've got a cat, and a boyfriend or two, and a job, and a few more independent ideas. I mean it's not as if you've taken up freefall parachuting or anything."

"I guess. I'm just thinking maybe I should start dropping some of this stuff into my letters. Sort of subtle-like. You know, to avoid any big head-on clash when I get back."

"Maybe you'll get a chance to work all this out sooner than you think."

"What do you mean?"

"Oh, we were going to try to surprise you."

"Aunt Caroline. I should probably tell you there's hardly anything on earth I hate more than surprises."

"She's coming here."

"My mother?"

"Yeah."

"When?"

"Tomorrow."

Chapter 13

Her mother was due in at 5:00, so Kate would have plenty of time to get home and change from jeans — which were what she wore to school almost all of the time now — into a dressier skirt and blouse outfit before going out to the airport with Aunt Caroline. Then they would bring her back to the house for dinner. Laura was going to fix Mexican chicken wings and anchovy fritters.

"Really, Laura. I don't want you to go to all that trouble. Why don't you just do a plain old roast and potatoes?"

"Oh no. This is a special occasion. I want to do it up a bit."

Kate couldn't think of any way to push it further and not insult Laura, so she just dropped it.

They got out to the airport half an hour early and sat down to wait on a bench by the gate.

"Are you excited?" Aunt Caroline asked her.

"More nervous."

"But excited too."

"I guess. I've really been too nervous to think about whether I'm excited or not. I guess I will be when she gets here."

"How long has it been?"

"Almost four months."

"She won't recognize you."

"That's one of the things I'm nervous about."

"Oh, I think she'll be pleased that you've lost a little weight and got your hair cut. I mean it's not like you've gotten tattooed or anything drastic."

"I know. I probably worry too much. It's just that I think she expects to find me looking just like I did when she last saw me. Changes of any kind don't usually go over too big with her."

"Must be a family trait. Frank's the same way. You know, it just occurred to me, you're going to be flying out of here pretty soon yourself."

"I know. I was thinking about that the other day."

"You must be happy. Oh, listen to me. I say, 'You must be happy to leave,' so you'll feel obliged to say, 'Oh no, Aunt Caroline, you've been so wonderful, I don't think I'll be able to bear to go.' Look, forget I said anything."

"Actually you have been wonderful. Sure I'm looking forward to going home and being with my mom and dad again, but I'll for sure miss you and Uncle Frank and Laura and all the neat stuff I've been doing here. I've been having an awful lot of fun here — more than before I came. The thing I'm not sure about is how much of the change is place and how much is inside me. I guess I'm just hoping I can transfer some of the new me I've found here back to Springville."

"Oh, I should think you'll be able to manage that. You know, you probably would've changed a lot this year no matter what. Maybe the change of scene accelerated things a little, but that's all."

"You think?"

"Would I lie to you?" Aunt Caroline said, then turned to look out the window. "Oh, oh, unless this is a very stray flying saucer, I think your mother's flight is coming in now."

"I don't see anything."

"Way off there. See the lights getting lower and lower. I'm a pretty good spotter."

Finally, the plane landed and taxied up to the gate and people were starting to come through the door. When it seemed

194

like the plane had emptied three times its capacity, Kate began to think maybe her mother had missed the flight. But then there she was. Kate almost didn't recognize her at first.

"You look so different," was all Kate could think of to say when all the waving, hugging, and kissing had subsided.

"So do you," her mother said.

"But your hair. And you're so dark."

"Well, the hair is a dye job I got on an extremely long, hot, and boring afternoon in Fort Myers, Florida. I'd already seen every movie playing in town and passed this beauty shop that said 'air conditioned — come on in,' and so I did. And the tan — well, the motel in Fort Myers had a pool and so that's where I've spent most of my days for the past five weeks. I guess I'm getting used to being a lady of leisure. The first month or so of this, I was restless. Now we get to a new place and I see all the movies, raid the bookstores, find a couple of good restaurants, do the museums, and then just give in to indolence and let the days pass until it's time to move on."

"We'd better get going," Aunt Caroline said. "Laura's got a big dinner waiting for us. Why don't you two go to the baggage claim and I'll bring the car around."

"It sounds sort of depressing," Kate told her mother while they were waiting for her bag. "This gypsy life, I mean."

"It was at first. I guess I've gotten used to it — used to being alone and having more time on my hands than usual. And I bought a camera. I've been taking a lot of pictures wherever we go. I'm getting pretty good too. When I get home, I'm going to sort them out and see what I've got. I'm thinking maybe somebody might be interested in them for a book. You know — sort of an on the road through America thing. My goodness, you're thin."

"I guess I've lost a little. They don't have a scale so I don't know how much. Do you like it?"

"I don't know. I liked you fine the way you were. I guess we can fatten you up a little when you get home. How're you feeling?"

"Oh, you know me. I'm always healthy as a horse."

"No, I meant how are you feeling. Are you getting along all right here? It's not getting you down too much?

"Oh no. It's fine."

"I wanted you to know how proud I am of you for bearing up so well. Even in your letters, you've managed to put on a cheery face."

"But really, I'm fine. Everything's fine."

"Good, good. I just wanted to let you know that I've been thinking about ways to make it up to you for having had to put you through all this. And I think I've come up with a pretty special treat."

"What?" Kate asked, abandoning any more attempts at making her mother understand that living with the Myers hadn't been at all cruel and unusual punishment. If her mother wanted to give her a treat in payment for all her supposed suffering, she was willing to play martyr to the hilt.

"Never you mind just now. It's a surprise. I'll let you know in plenty of time."

Dinner was lots of fun. Kate just sat back and watched her mother try to politely turn down a second helping of anchovy fritters and ignore the dogs eating loudly out of their bowls at the far end of the table (a recent scheme of Aunt Caroline's to make them feel more a part of the family). Cardigan, who was welcome to eat with the dogs but preferred his old plate on the floor, came through the kitchen a couple of times, but her mother didn't focus in on him. Kate planned to introduce him to her mother later that night, after things had settled down a bit and she had a chance to prepare her.

Laura was especially yakky, even for her, and told Kate's mother of her plans for her move to New York. Her mother's response was polite, but with that slight arch of the eyebrow that was a dead giveaway — to Kate at least — that she saw it as being about half a step away from a move to Sodom and Gommorah. As soon as they finished eating, Laura hopped up from the table and announced that she was going over to Bob's to study for a test.

"Don't wait up. I'm so far behind in this class, it may take us until 2 A.M. to get me caught up."

"Won't you be bothering his parents — staying that late?" Kate's mother asked. Kate knew that Bob's parents' sound sleep was not what she was concerned about.

"Oh, no. We study up in his bedroom. I don't think they even know we're up there."

Kate was loving all this. If the Meyers had been conspiring to shock her mother, they couldn't have done a better job. By the time she got around to focusing in on Kate's minor changes, she would probably be ready to accept Kate bringing a pet orangutan home with her, dating married men, and going to work as a cocktail waitress. Or so Kate thought until they got up to her room later that night.

"What a nice, cozy place," Kate's mother

said, looking around, taking in without more comment the place Kate had spent two hours cleaning and straightening up the night before.

"Well, I don't know about cozy. You could store about six elephants up here."

"Well, cozy in atmosphere, if not in size then. Who's this? One of your classmates?"

Of all the stupid things. Kate had spent two hours going over the room with a fine tooth comb last night — cleaning and straightening up, and hiding her make-up box, and the stack of Gothic romances, and with all that, she managed to leave the wallet-sized senior picture of Andy stuck in the frame of her dresser mirror. Andy, the "classmate" who had written "Love ya, babe" across the bottom right-hand corner.

And so the confrontation Kate had most been dreading began.

"Yeah," she said. "He's just a guy from school."

"Seems like he knows you pretty well."

"We go out sometimes. You know."

"No I don't. I didn't know you went out with boys at all. Caroline's been letting you date?"

"Well, sort of."

"Why didn't you mention it in your letters?"

"I guess it must have slipped my mind."

"Do you expect me to believe that?"

"It really isn't any kind of big deal. I mean I don't have guys lined up around the block. I only go out with the one in the picture and another guy. And I'm not really serious about either of them. They're both nice. Aunt Caroline knows them both and thinks they're fine. I was going to tell you about this. I just didn't want to put it all in a letter. I guess I was afraid you'd think there was more to it than there is, and get upset. Are you? Upset I mean?"

"Well, I'm certainly upset that you've been keeping things from me, whatever the reason. Am I upset that you have a boyfriend — two boyfriends? I don't know. I guess I shouldn't be. You are sixteen after all. I guess I'm just a little startled to find out all this has been going on without my knowledge. I sort of thought this was something that would happen gradually. When you were back home. Something we'd talk over. Boys Dad and I would meet. Not that I don't trust Caroline's judgment. I guess I just feel like you've gone and grown up and have this whole new life I don't know anything about."

"Well, who sent me off to this whole new life?"

"Are you still playing Cinderella about

all this? You know, I'm not the wicked stepmother who cast you into the cellar to peel potatoes for seven months. You're just a victim of circumstances, Kate. There is no villainess in this piece and I'm tired of your trying to make me into one."

"Oh, I'm over that. All I meant was that I don't see how you can expect to ship me off — no matter how sensible the reasons — to a completely new place, leave me there for several months to fend for myself, and not expect some changes."

"You say *some* changes. Are there more surprises in store for me?"

"No. Well, a couple of little ones."

"Like?"

"Well, one's crouching over in the far corner there."

Kate watched as her mother walked over and from a very safe distance eyeballed Cardigan, who, showing more sense than she thought he had, sat very still and eyeballed her mother back. After about a minute of this stand-off, Cardigan gave in, rolled over on his back and went into a move that looked like he was pedalling an upside-down, invisible cat bicycle.

"Why's he doing that?" her mother asked.

"He wants you to scratch his stomach and pet him a little."

"He'll get awfully tired waiting for that."

"You don't like him?"

"It's nothing personal. As cats go, he seems fine. It's just that I find all cats generally loathesome."

"Then I can't keep him?"

"You mean bring him back home? I should say not!"

"But I'd take care of him, and feed him, and keep him out of your way. I promise. He's used to me. It'd break his little heart if I just left him here."

"Well, he'll just have to get over it because he's not coming to my house. Now that you know that — and I can't imagine how you ever kidded yourself into thinking I'd ever let you have a cat — you can start breaking it to him gently."

"How can you break something gently to a cat?"

"Well, that's your problem. You should have thought of this earlier. Like before you got him."

"But I didn't get him. Aunt Caroline did, then gave him to me. I really didn't have anything to say about it at all in the beginning. Now when I'm real attached to him, you tell me I'm just going to have to dump him. It isn't fair."

"Lots of things aren't fair. Life isn't

fair. It's probably time you started learning that."

Kate went over and picked up Cardigan and brought him back to her bed. She sat there petting him, trying to think of something to say in his defense. Her mother sat down on Kate's desk chair.

"So what else is new?" she asked, as if to dismiss the cat as a closed subject.

"Nothing." It didn't seem like quite the right time to tell her about the cleaners job.

"How's school?"

"It's okay."

"Kate. I'm here to talk with you, not to interview you."

"Really, there's just not anything to tell."

"Look. I'm dead tired. This has been a long day. I don't really feel like sitting here asking you questions and getting two- and three-syllable answers. I'll go to bed. Maybe by tomorrow you'll be done sulking. I wanted to take you shopping. Why don't you let me know how you feel about that in the morning."

"But tomorrow's a school day."

"I thought, seeing as it's the only day I'll be here, you might take off. Of course, if you'd rather not . . ."

"Oh, no. I'd always rather go shopping than go to school." Kate knew that what she was supposed to say was something about how much she wanted to spend the day with her mother, but she just wasn't going to give her the satisfaction. It wasn't so much her not letting Kate keep Cardigan, but the crummy way she did it, with so little concern for Kate's feelings. The way Kate figured it, she had to go back home, wanted to go. And it was her parents' home. And she loved both of them and was willing to follow their rules. But following the rules didn't mean she had to like them.

And so she watched her mother go down the stairs without saying good night. As she undressed for bed, she began cooking up a scheme to get Lucy to take Cardigan so she could at least visit him. Then in a year, when she got to college, maybe she could have him back again.

At least her mother hadn't said anything about her not dating when she got back home. Of course, she hadn't said anything about her dating when she got back home either. But then back home was another place. Maybe no one would ask her and it would be a moot point. Kate thought she could probably afford to put that off until it became a real issue.

Kate thought the shopping trip would smooth things over between them. How could she have predicted that it would turn into yet another battle of wills? Before, shopping had been one of the most fun things they did together. Of course, that had been back when Kate just let her mother decide what kind of clothes Kate needed, which styles suited her best, which items were the most well-made and durable. Now that Kate had been picking her own things for a while, she wanted more than just being a mannequin to show off her mother's taste.

The item of contention was a red and blue jumper, well-made, styleless enough to be serviceable for years, and a good buy. The only problem was that Kate hated it and knew that no matter how long she lived, there would never come a day when she would willingly wear it.

"It's lovely," her mother gushed as she fluttered around Kate in the fitting room.

"It is, isn't it?" Kate said, choosing her words carefully. "But do you think it's me?"

"What do you mean, is it you? It fits perfectly."

"Well, it's just that it's not quite what the girls around here are wearing."

"What do you care? You're not going to be around here much longer."

"That's another thing. I'm not really

sure what they're wearing in Springville now. I think maybe I ought to wait until I get back before I buy a lot of stuff."

"This isn't a lot of stuff. This is one perfectly lovely, classic jumper that'll be in style for years and fashionable anywhere from here to Paris."

Kate thought of giving in, saying she loved it, and letting her mother tell the salesgirl to wrap it up. For sure that would be the easiest way out. The last thing she wanted to do was start up a fight with her on the one day they'd had together in so many months. On the other hand, it seemed sort of short-sighted to buy the jumper now when she knew she would never be able to bring herself to wear it. It was so babyish looking — like something you'd wear with leggings and a lunch box. Of course, she could just let her mother buy it today, then when she got home say it had gotten lost at the cleaners or something, but she was a terrible liar. But what really decided her on forcing the issue was something completely aside from all this logic — something she didn't quite understand that made it seem very important for her to assert herself and tell her mother she didn't want the dress.

"I don't want it."

"What?"

"I mean it's real nice and all, but it's just not quite my style and I probably wouldn't wear it much if I got it. I wanted to be honest about it so you wouldn't spend your money needlessly."

"I see."

"I didn't mean to offend you or anything."

"Just what is your taste these days? You'll have to pardon my ignorance, but I wasn't aware that you had strong taste in clothes."

"Well, I guess I'm starting to get some ideas of my own. Like those sundresses we saw in the other department."

"Kate, they're so cheap looking."

"Well, they're just for summer. They're just to kick around in. Nobody expects a sundress to look expensive. Unless you're wearing it on a yacht, I guess."

A long time — or at least what seemed like a long time to Kate — went by without either of them saying anything. Finally, her mother picked her purse up off the fitting-room bench.

"I guess I just wasn't prepared for this."

"For me wanting to get a sundress?"

"Come on. For your being so changed. There's nothing wrong with your wanting a sundress. Or even not wanting a jumper I like. I know that. It's just that it's not the kind of thing you would have fought me on before. Actually, I can't remember you ever fighting me on much of anything before. Your whole attitude has changed so much. You *have* an attitude now. And opinions. You seem so *independent*."

"Is that so bad?"

"Well, I've grown used to your being dependent on me. On the other hand, I do want you to be an independent adult. I guess you just started to make the transition here and I've come in on the middle of it and so it's a little scary. But I think I'll adjust. I'll try anyway. Now. Why don't you get dressed and meet me over by the sundresses. Let's see if we can find something decent."

"Mom?"

"What?"

"Thanks."

As she got back into her clothes, Kate felt flushed with good feelings. Part of them were toward her mother for giving in so gracefully. But most of them were for herself. It wasn't just that she was going to get a cool sundress instead of a turkey jumper. Much more important was that her mother saw that she was changing and had acknowledged and at least made a start at accepting it. And most important, for one of the first times in her life, she had had the nerve to stand up and say, "I am not nobody. I am me." And somebody had listened and said, "Why, yes, I guess you are."

Chapter 14

Kate was in the laundry room late that night after taking her mother to the airport. She was ironing a shirt for the next day when Laura — just getting in — poked her head through the door.

"Hey. How'd it go?" she asked.

"Okay."

"It didn't look to me like you were having such an awful time or were real nervous or anything."

"No. It turned out to be pretty jolly. I knew it would be fun to see her. I was just worried about dumping a whole lot of new stuff on her at once and how she would take it. Mostly it went better than I expected. There *were* a few snags, though."

"Yeah, Mom told me you won't get to keep the kitten."

"I'm working out a scheme on that. As for the rest, well, I think her coming was a good thing. Now I don't think she expects to get back exactly the same kid she shipped off. I mean I know I'll have to toe the line a little more there than I do here, but I think I paved the way for negotiations. It used to be they'd hand down the rules from on high and I'd bow and obey. I was worried that I couldn't go back to that. Now I don't think I'll have to."

"What did the surprise turn out to be?"

"Oh, it's a good one. The last branch office my Dad has to go to is in Los Angeles. That'll be after school is out here and so they want me to meet them there. My mom'll take me to Disneyland, and Knott's Berry Farm, and on the bus tour of the homes of the stars. All the corny tourist stuff. We'll have about a month there and so I should be able to spend a lot of time on the beach. Maybe learn to surf."

"Hey neat!"

"It sounds like it, doesn't it? Where've you been? Was there rehearsal tonight?"

"I guess I forgot to tell you. I got snagged into being on the prom committee."

"The prom? Isn't that still light years away?"

"Oh, I know. It's not until the end of May. You'd think it was next weekend, though, to listen to them at this meeting — how much there is to do and how we've really got to get cracking. Of course with how long it takes them to agree on every small point, the prom will probably have to be moved back to August. This meeting tonight lasted three hours and all we did was decide on the theme and the flavor of the punch."

"Don't keep me in suspense."

"Well, the theme is 'Silver Sands' — sort of a Polynesian number. You know. Mostly what it means is that the basketball nets in the gym will be hidden behind fake coconut trees. And the punch flavor, astoundingly enough, will be Hawaiian Fruit."

"Is the prom a big deal around here?"

"I'd say most kids around here see the three great events in their life as birth, death, and the prom, and not necessarily in that order."

"Then I guess I ought to start worrying tonight about whether anyone's going to ask me."

"Oh, Andy'll ask you for sure."

"Nothing's for sure with Andy."

"Have you figured out yet what makes that boy tick?"

"I don't know. I think he's a lot less mysterious than he seems. He's not all that bright for one thing. I don't mean he's a moron or anything. It's just that he's not a real heavy thinker. I think he operates mostly on gut reactions and impulses. Like he thinks I'm smart and funny and so when he wants to talk, or when he's up for fooling around, he calls me. Then when he wants to show up somewhere with a knockout on his arm, or when he just wants to go out to the bluff and park for four hours, he calls Kim. I mean, I like to go up there at the end of the night. You know. We can talk in private, and make out a little, and it seems like a special time just for us. But once he took me up there for the whole night and I wound up playing maulee to his mauler. I don't like to have to fight him off and so I told him I don't want to get into situations where I will. I figure let Kim have him on his werewolf nights."

"But do you like him?"

"I do, desperately. Then I don't at all. Then I think I like him too much for how much he seems to like me. Then I wonder why I like him so little when, in most of the ways that count, he's really terrific. Actually, I think a good part of how much I like him doesn't have a whole lot to do with him at all. Or at least it has more to do with how I feel being with him. Going out with him. Being seen with him. As you know, before I came here . . . well, if I'd kept a diary, most of the pages would be blank. He's really my first boyfriend. And so aside from what he is or isn't, I like just *having* a boyfriend. It makes me feel like a different person. And I like being close enough with a boy that I can talk to him for real. You know, beyond nervous small talk. You can see this isn't the most coherent set of thoughts. Anyway, the whole thing is probably going to be a moot point in a couple of months. I mean, I can't really imagine him taking the Greyhound every weekend to see me."

"I never thought about it before, but you're sort of in the same position I am with Bob — a terminal romance, one that has an end in sight. In a way, it kind of makes it easier, doesn't it?"

"How do you mean?"

"Well, when I decided for sure to go to New York, all the whim whams I'd been having about whether or not I wanted to marry Bob, well they sort of flew out the window. Now I know we only have until the fall and so I've quit worrying about him and me and just enjoy it for what it is now."

"Yeah, I guess that's sort of where I am too."

"You know, I think he will ask you to the prom."

He didn't. He asked Kim Thomas. Kate heard her on the other side of the lockers after gym class one day asking one of her friends if she and her boyfriend wanted to double with them. Kate knew that Kim knew she was in the room and that she was probably gushing on about what color tux Andy would probably wear, and how she mustn't forget to get him a boutonniere, and where they were planning to go for dinner afterward, all just to get the message across to Kate. Well, score one for Kim.

She guessed she couldn't really blame him. He knew she was leaving soon. Taking her to the prom would have been a nice parting gesture. Taking Kim was an investment in the future. At least in a good summer. She told herself a hundred times not to let it bother her. What was one dumb night, dancing around the same old gym she did calisthenics in every week? And this way she'd save all the money she would have had to blow on a dress she would only wear one night. And she would free herself from weeks of worry about what a klutz she was going to look like out on the dance floor.

What she couldn't understand was why, after telling herself all these rational, and objective and true things, she still felt miserable that he hadn't asked her.

This sort of thing happened a lot lately — either getting bothered by something like this that really didn't seem worth bothering about, or not being bothered by something that she really ought to be bothered about. Like how she hated Mr. Schenkel and his geometry class and hadn't done any work in it in three weeks and was sure to flunk. As it would be her first F ever, her parents were sure to go through the roof when they found out. Logically, this was something to be worried about, but strangely enough she couldn't care less.

It was like someone far off at a control panel somewhere was handling her emotions. She could never predict a second in advance how she was going to feel about anything. The only thing for sure was that whatever she felt was going to be at the furthest end of some spectrum. Wildly happy, or excruciatingly miserable, or, like about the geometry class, giddily nonchalant. She didn't seem to have any nice, calm, stable middle ground anymore. She mentioned this to Aunt Caroline one night.

All she said was: "I think you lose your middle ground around fifteen and don't get it back until around thirty."

Kate couldn't tell if she was serious. She hoped not. Fourteen more years on this rollercoaster and she would probably be a basket case.

Two weeks before the prom — predictably, as it was equivalent to one night's notice before a weekend date — Dave Kruger called and asked her if she wanted to go with him. By this time, she had been made so miserable for so many weeks listening to Laura and everyone else making elaborate prom night plans that an invitation had begun to seem as desirable and unattainable as winning the Miss America pageant or a Nobel Prize.

She had even had it in the back of her mind for a couple of weeks now that Dave might call. She knew he wouldn't ask anyone else, but it wasn't unfeasible that he just might not look up from his electronic one-man band — his current project — until the prom was about two weeks past. All along, she had figured that if he did call, she would say yes. And so she was completely surprised when she heard herself telling him she would love to but she just couldn't because she had already planned to go shopping in Chicago with her Aunt that weekend. It was a total lie. And to make matters worse, Aunt Caroline passed through the front hall by the phone just as she was telling it.

After she hung up, Aunt Caroline came out of the kitchen and said: "You'd better remind me to get the points and plugs tuned up before we drive up to Chicago."

"I'm sorry you heard that. I'd rather people didn't know how stupidly I run my life."

"Why did you do it?"

"I'm not sure. I'm not sure why I do a lot of things I do lately. As close as I can tell, the whole thing just started seeming dumb to me — going with a guy I really don't care about just to go to the prom. And unfair to him too. You know. He'd have to rent a tux, and pay for the tickets, and pop for an expensive dinner. If he goes, it should be with someone who's going to be with him, not just to be there. Does that make any sense?"

"Sounds like it makes very good sense. Now, what about Chicago?"

"Oh, that was just the first excuse I could think of."

"Seems to me if you said you were going to be in Chicago that weekend, you'd better be in Chicago that weekend. You don't want to get caught out in a lie."

"Oh, I can just lie low around here. I doubt that he's going to come by with a searchlight."

"No, really. Why don't we go? I promised you the trip a long time ago. The prom weekend's as good as any. What do you say? I'll even spring for the hotel, and meals, and stuff. Have you socked away any money from the cleaners so you can get some clothes?"

"I've got almost $150 now. I'll have more by the time we go."

"Good. So what do you say?"

"I think I'm going to enter you in the 'Aunt of the Year' contest."

The trip turned out to be the most fun Kate had ever had in the concentrated space of two days. She and Aunt Caroline left after school on Friday and got to their hotel just after 8:00 that night. From their room, Aunt Caroline called her old college roommate, Agnes, whom they were supposed to meet for dinner.

For some reason, Kate had expected restaurants in Chicago to be big and fancy with white tablecloths and vases of rosebuds. And so she was surprised when the address they had given the cab driver turned out to be a slightly run-down-looking bar between a locksmith and a lighting fixture store.

Agnes — "Just call me Agnes," she had told Kate right off and so she never did find out her whole name — was waiting out front for them when they pulled up.

"We have to go through here to get to the garden," she told them after she and Aunt Caroline had gone through much hugging and oohing and ahhing over how young the other one looked, while Kate stood around wondering what the age was when a person started wanting to be told they looked younger than they were.

Then they went through the bar, which had panelled walls lined with three or four pinball machines and a ceiling hung with maybe twenty piñatas, and out onto an enclosed patio with a dozen round metal tables. Agnes and Aunt Caroline had margaritas while Kate had a Coke. Then they all shared orders of guacamole, and tostadas, and burritos, none of which was like anything Kate had ever eaten before and all of which was real good.

Agnes and Aunt Caroline mostly talked about stuff they had done in college, stuff that seemed funnier and funnier to them as they progressed through three margaritas apiece. Kate didn't mind that they weren't paying much attention to her. Some of the stories were interesting, and when they weren't, she occupied herself watching people at other tables. Most of them were young and hip looking and their conversations — from what Kate could overhear — were smart and funny and about books, and movies, and stuff she couldn't get people to talk about enough. Maybe, she thought, she could go to college in Chicago.

She could ask Mrs. Hepple, the guidance counselor, about it when she went back to school in the fall.

Saturday morning they got up, had breakfast in the hotel coffee shop, and shopped for the rest of the day until late afternoon. Back in Port Williams, all Kate had thought about Chicago was that it would be a neat place to shop — full of good stores and stuff they weren't even thinking about wearing yet back home. Now, walking through Marshall Field's and on up Michigan Avenue, she could hardly think about the shopping for all there was to see — the skyscrapers, and traffic, and the crush of people, all kinds of people from bums to designer-dressed models (or at least so thin and chic, Kate figured they *had* to be models). At least a dozen times during the afternoon, she found herself caught up in wondering what it would be like to live in a place like this, where so much was happening all the time.

Still, between all her fantasies of what it would be like to be grown up and on her own in a big city, she did manage to focus in on the business at hand enough to collect two new shirts, a pair of jeans, a canvas shoulder bag, and a box of very classy stationery with no little "K's" in the corners.

After going back to the hotel for a nap and a change of clothes, she and Aunt Caroline took a cab to the near north side for dinner at a French restaurant that was so fancy she was glad they brought the check face down to Aunt Caroline so she didn't have to think too much about what the meal had cost.

"Maybe we should've just gone to Stouffer's or something," Kate said.

"Why?"

"Well, I don't want you to go broke treating me."

"Hey, it's a treat for me too, you know. I haven't had so much fun in a long time. I was wondering if I should have bought that pantsuit. You do think it's special, though, don't you?"

"Oh, yes," Kate said, flattered that Aunt Caroline really seemed to care about her opinion. At the moment everything — the day and the city and the swankiness of the restaurant and the glass of Aunt Caroline's wine that they had shared — was conspiring to make her feel like an adult. Until now, being grown up had mostly seemed a scary proposition. And so she was a little surprised at how easy it was and how good it felt.

After dinner, they went downtown to see a play that turned out to be so terrible, she and Aunt Caroline cracked up all through it, even in places you could tell weren't supposed to be funny.

"Goodness," Aunt Caroline said as they were coming out, "I hope Laura doesn't starve for five years out in New York just to get into something as bad as this."

Sunday they went to the Art Institute, looked around for a couple of hours, then had lunch in the garden there. Afterward, Aunt Caroline sat out in the lobby and waited patiently for the half hour or so it took Kate to decide on which postcards to get in the gift shop there. She had this idea of putting together a collection of cards of Impressionist paintings, which were the ones she had liked best today, and taping them up on the wall behind her bed at home.

When she got done, Aunt Caroline told her it was time to go.

"So we can be home in time for dinner?"

"Well actually, it's more that I'm down to my last ten dollars. I figure that's enough for gas. If the car breaks down, you'll have to push us the rest of the way to Port Williams."

On the way home, they talked a while and laughed a lot about all the things they had seen and done that weekend. Then, driving through the monotonous miles of farmland, Kate drifted off into her own private stream of thoughts.

The newness of all the experiences she had had in Chicago made her think about the possibilities of new places in general. She thought about all the differences just these few months in Port Williams had made in who she was and how she looked at things. And there was California just around the corner, which was bound to be a whole other set of experiences. And then college in a year. Somehow, considering all this made going back to Springville seem not so much of a dead end.

Even if she got back there and no one asked her out, and her mother clamped on all the old rules, and Lucy and the gang were too wrapped up in their romances to find time for her — even at the very worst, it was only for a year. Even if she were still the old Kate, she could live that year on memories of the good times she had had here and in anticipation of the good times to come in college. But she wasn't the old Kate. She was a new and different and better person, and somehow she knew that was going to make things back home new and different and better for her.

As usual, the result of all this deep thinking was that she fell asleep. When she woke up, they were only about forty-five minutes from home.

When they got in, Laura was just starting dinner and wanted to hear all about the trip, and so they sat around talking to her while she worked. Kate picked up and sniffed at Laura's prom corsage, which had been laying on the table, and was amazed at not feeling a single pang of regret.

Chapter 15

The next Sunday, the morning after the last smash performance of *The Little Foxes*, and the late-night cast and crew party to which Kate had asked Dave Kruger to smooth out any possible hard feelings about turning down his prom invitation, Andy called at 9 A.M., getting an extremely bleary-eyed Kate out of bed.

"Have you been outside yet?" he asked.

"I haven't even woken up yet."

"Well, go out on the front porch."

"Have you lost your mind?"

"Maybe. Now will you just go out on the front porch?"

"Okay. Okay."

She went and pushed open the screen door and found, right in front of it, a toy sand pail and shovel. Taped to the side of the pail was a note. She opened it and read:

"I got up at seven, discovered that summer had arrived overnight, and wondered if you'd spend the first day of it with me at the beach."

226

She got back on the phone and asked him, "How soon can you pick me up?"

"What if I give you time to wake up, and have breakfast, and find your sun tan oil? Say an hour?"

"You're on."

As it turned out, they didn't get started until around 11:30. Andy called back once to say his dad was making him mow the lawn before he left, then again to say he was going to stop by to get some Cokes and could she maybe make up some sandwiches and did she have a beach blanket because his mother couldn't find theirs.

And so, when they finally got out to the lake, the beach was packed. Which was great because the main reason to go to Crystal Lake, and to Fred's Beach in particular, was because everyone else did. As far as Kate could tell, everyone in both the junior and senior classes was there (except Laura and Bob and they were planning to drive out as soon as he finished replacing his carburetor) — all oiled up and spread out on beach towels and blankets. Or setting up grills to cook hot dogs and hamburgers. Or having chicken fights out where the lake turned from light to dark blue and got chest high. Or getting covered with sand, playing volleyball. About fifty radios were blaring, but as they were all tuned to the one decent rock station in Port Williams, the music made it seem as if everyone, whether they knew each other or not, was part of one giant party.

The first thing they did was scan the crowd for Bill.

"We've got to find him," Andy said. "After all, he has the frisbee."

They finally spotted him down near the water on a cluster of blankets with a bunch of kids Kate vaguely knew in the way she now vaguely knew a lot of kids at PW High. Weaving between bodies, tripping over coolers, they made their way slowly down to the shoreline. Bill spotted them coming.

"Hey," he said as they dumped their stuff down on the sand, "can you believe this? It's like everybody got up this morning and simultaneously had the same great idea. Or maybe the Martians landed last night and put implants in everyone's brain — you know, like in the science fiction movies — and sent the same signal to everyone between fifteen and eighteen. GO TO BEACH."

And so the afternoon melted away for Kate, so that by the time the sun started pulling away to the edge of the horizon, she couldn't really tell how long she had been out there. Or how many times she had been in and out of the water with Andy teasing her about how she didn't have to worry about not knowing how to swim, that he would save her if she started to drown, then following close behind, sneaking up to her underwater, and leaping up and grabbing her into a splash-surrounded kiss. Or how many hot dogs she had eaten, how many Cokes she had drunk. Or where she had gotten the scrape on the bottom of her foot.

The low point of the afternoon came late when she and Andy were collapsed on the blanket, drying themselves off in the fading rays. Kate felt a shadow looming over her, looked up, and saw Kim Thomas, shaking the water out of her long blond hair, gently nudging Andy in the ribs with her foot.

"Hey, fella, Want to throw the frisbee around with me for a while?"

This was quickly followed by the high point of the day when he rolled over, yawned exaggeratedly and said, "Thanks, but I was just going to get Kate to take a little walk down the beach with me."

With that he grabbed her hand, stood up, and yanked her off the blanket and started running down the beach, away from the crowd, half dragging her behind him.

When they got to a deserted cove between some rocks, he dropped to the sand, bringing her down with him, grabbing her around the waist, rolling the two of them over once, twice, three times until they wound up lying suddenly still side by side.

"You could've played frisbee with her," Kate told him. "I wouldn't have minded."

"Yeah, but I would've. You're leaving in a couple of weeks. Kim'll be around here forever. Which reminds me of something I wanted to explain to you."

"You don't owe me any explanations."

"Maybe. But I'll feel a lot better if I get this off my chest. It's about the prom."

"In that case, you really don't owe me any explanations. If you'd asked me, I would've never got to go to Chicago."

"Ouch. You really know how to hurt a guy. Would you really rather go to Chicago than go to the prom with a terrific guy like me?"

"You think I'd give you the satisfaction of answering that?"

"See, you do think I'm a rotten crumb. I knew it. Well, I wanted to let you know I'm not. I thought about it a lot beforehand. What I wanted to do was take you. That's the truth whether you believe it or not. Then one night I was out with Kim and a bunch of kids. Something she said to one of her girlfriends — I can't remember what it was — made me realize what a big deal it was to her. She hasn't really been going out much with anyone but me lately. I mean if I didn't ask her, nobody would. She's lived in this town all her life and probably always will. All her friends were going and talking it up all the time and I knew if she didn't get to go she'd be crushed. You, well you're going to go back home real soon. You'll probably forget all about this place and never see any of these kids again. And next year you'll be a senior and have your own prom to go to."

"If anybody asks me."

"Oh, they will. You'll probably have a line-up to pick from. I'll even make a deal with you. If nobody better asks you, I'd love to come out to Springville and take you myself. I look pretty good in a tux."

"I may take you up on that."

"Well, I mean it. Hey, maybe we could write each other once in a while."

"Sure."

"That was a disbelieving 'sure' if I ever heard one. You don't think I'm going to write at all, do you?"

"No."

"Well, that shows you how much you know. I am actually a pretty good letter writer. I write my Uncle Herb twice a year — once in the summer and at Christmas, and I write both my grandmothers on their birthdays. And those are people I don't even care about writing to. Think how much better I'm bound to do with you — a person I really do want to write to."

"Well, if you write me, I'll for sure write back. But I'll have to see that first letter to believe it."

"Do you believe I love you?"

"Not really."

"Sensible girl. Really, though, in my own half-baked way, I think I do. If you were staying here, I think it might be different. Knowing that you were going to be leaving, that this would have to end, well, it didn't seem smart to let things go too far."

"I know what you mean."

"But I really would like to keep in touch. Find out where you're going to go to college. Maybe we'll wind up at the same place."

"Have you made up your mind about that?"

"More or less. I guess I'm going to try to keep my dad happy and give it a shot at State. It's a little late, but I think I can still get a swimming scholarship there."

"I think you'll have a better time than you would hanging around here. By the fall, almost everybody's going to be gone anyway."

"That's sort of what I was thinking. Hey, if you don't believe I love you, do you believe something else?"

"What?"

"That I really want to kiss you right now?"

Kate laughed. *"That* I do believe."

And so they did — long and hard, lost in the warm sand beneath them, and the salty taste, and Coppertone smell of each other. Until they heard the click of a Polaroid, followed by Bill's cackling laughter.

It took Andy fifteen minutes to chase him down and wrest the picture out of his clutches. When he came back, he dropped it onto the sand next to her.

"I think you'd better take this for safekeeping."

And so she did. And kept it in the zippered side pocket of her suitcase the whole time in California. And then in the bottom drawer under all her sweaters when she got home. And for a long time, just knowing it was there — her best secret — made her smile whenever she thought about it. She saved actually getting it out and looking at it for the worst days. The days nothing outside her was going right, or when everything inside her seemed all muddled up. The days when the new Kate seemed to be slipping out from underneath her. In these down moments, the photo was the proof she needed that the new Kate was alive and well and going to be around for some time to come.